BORN OF LIES

A prequel to the Red Ridge Pack series

By Sara Dailey and Staci Weber

The world changed for Lillian Michaels the day Marcus chose her. Gorgeous, strong fierce…and soon he would be alpha of her werewolf pack. But then the marriage was set. No choice. No looking back. Except, she did. Lillian started looking forward, too, and wondering if eighteen was too young to give away her life.

Certainly, it is tonight. A rock concert. She and her friend, intoxicating music, sweat, bodies, freedom…and *him*: Paul. The human bassist's touch makes her soul sing like the strings of his axe, and everything is possible. Yet, Lillian's parents, her secrets, her entire world lies elsewhere. Paul doesn't even see what she is, what she can do. What she *must* do. This to-die-for human is not of her kind. And yet, something special, something terrifyingly perfect, something eternally true has been…

BORN OF LIES

A prequel to the Red Ridge Pack series

By Sara Dailey and Staci Weber

www.BOROUGHSPUBLISHINGGROUP.com

BORN OF LIES

ISBN: 978-1-941260-52-4

For St. Agnes Academy's Class of 1994 and Sam Rayburn High School's Class of 1998.

Thanks for the awesome memories.

Never lost shall I be, my love

For within you, I will forever dwell

Misery, mine eyes have touched

Until you

Crooked paths shall never lead me asunder

All roads lead to the shine of your gaze

The beat of your core

This moment, this breath, this place

'Tis all for you my darling, my great never-ending

For there is no darkness in which I cannot find you

You are my freedom.

—Jordan Mantell

Contents

Prologue

Christmas morning, 2012

This can't be happening is stuck on a loop in my head as I stare at the man standing in my doorway. I ran away from Marcus Walker, the alpha of our pack, all those years ago to save myself. Paul and I came back to the pack to save our daughter Alli. Now, would our son be sacrificed because of the mistakes I made? The choices I made?

My mind can hardly wrap itself around the words coming from the mouth of the man I once thought I loved. Completely shocked, I tear my eyes away from Marcus and look at my oldest child Aiden, trying to gauge his reaction.

Marcus now knows Aiden is his biological son. His firstborn. Marcus's other son Cade has been prepped for the role of alpha since birth, and Cade doesn't plan on giving up the position without a fight.

Alli is mated to Cade. Now that Marcus has learned that the pack is in danger, he expects the two brothers to make a choice. Take a stand.

His voice is a deep, low rumble. "Fight it out if you have to, but I need one of you to step up."

My motherly instincts demand that I slam the door in his smug face, but the wolf inside me doesn't allow it. He may be a tyrant, but he is our alpha, and whether I like it or not, the father of my oldest child. None of this is up to Paul and me.

My past has finally caught up with me, and this time, there really is nothing I can do about it. Both my children will pay for the choices I made.

Chapter 1

May 1994

"Hey, Lily, hold up for a sec," Tiffany yelled in her infamously brash tone, which never fails to catch the attention of everyone in a mile radius. A group of stoners immediately turned to look my way. In very Tiffany-fashion, she threw her hands up at them and said, "Mind your own business, losers."

Trying to cover the embarrassment that goes hand-in-hand with Tiffany's uncensored comments, I avoided eye contact with the onlookers and stood by the wall in the hallway to wait. Tiffany was apparently overseeing the purchase of her ticket to the Red Ridge High Class of 1994's senior prom. Her date, Jason, handed the cashier a wad of bills, and after the tickets were in his hands, she kissed him on the cheek and said, "Later, baby."

As she bounced my way, I tried my best not to appear jealous, but I was. I'd dreamed of my prom night since my freshman year, but since my boyfriend Marcus decided it was lame and refused to be seen there I knew it would remain just that. A dream. One that would never come true.

"'Happily Ever After'... Can you say cheesy?" Tiffany announced to everyone within earshot. I just smiled, especially since I secretly thought it was the perfect theme. As we made our way toward first period, she asked, "So did you ever talk Marcus into taking you?"

"No. It's fine though. It's no big deal." I tried to act indifferent, but I knew she'd see right through me.

Tiffany and I didn't hang out much anymore, but we'd known each other our whole lives since we were both pack girls. We'd grown apart over the last year or so, but she still knew me better than most. She kind of had a wild streak, always hanging out with domestics and going to parties off the estate. Marcus didn't approve of her "lifestyle."

We sat down and class began. We were supposed to be discussing today's current event when in the middle of a sentence Tiffany totally switched gears and said, "Just come to prom with me. I know you've always wanted to go. You used to go on and on about it." At first I was shocked that she would even ask me, but then I figured she was just being nice since she knew that if Marcus wasn't going there was no way I could go.

"Seriously, it's just me, Jason, and a few others. They're not pack, but who cares. Come on, ditch Mr. Perfect for once and come out with us. You're going to regret it if you don't," she prodded again.

She was right. I would regret it, but Marcus would never allow me to go without him.

"It's really sweet of you to ask, Tiff, but you know I can't go without Marcus. But I'm going to talk to him again tonight about it. Maybe I can convince him," I replied, but knew the chances of that were slim to none.

Thankfully, Tiffany dropped the subject. We went back to talking about how the FBI now considered Russian organized crime one of the greatest threats to the US just as the teacher passed by our desks to check on our progress. I was off the hook…for now.

*****

I wanted to bring up prom on the way home from school, but I didn't need to start another argument with Marcus. Lately, it seemed that all we did was argue, and the last time we did anything fun was a distant memory. I was so nervous about approaching the topic again that my knuckles were sore from repeatedly popping them. It was a stupid nervous habit, and one that Marcus was fully aware of.

"What's going on, Lily?"

I turned slightly in my seat so I could gauge his reaction as he drove. "I really, really want to go to prom." Immediately Marcus rolled his eyes and shot me a look that made me feel pathetic, but I wasn't ready to give up just yet. "You always hear about people that don't go, and then when they're old they regret it. I don't want to regret not going. Do you?" I asked.

"The difference is that those people are domestics, and from what I can tell, humans regret a lot of things. Anyway, I thought this was over, Lily. Prom is tomorrow for Christ's sake. I don't want to hang out with a bunch of domestics all night. It's not natural. You know the risks involved with us just going to school with them."

The topic was closed, so I turned back around in my seat and waited for the rest of the lecture that was sure to come.

"What if some stupid domestic starts something and one of us can't control ourselves? Do you want the death of humans on your conscience? You are aware of what would happen if someone found out about us, aren't you?"

That was Marcus's go-to excuse for avoiding humans at all costs, but it was a load of crap. No eighteen-year-old guy, werewolf or not, was that freaking paranoid. The truth was he just didn't want to associate with domestics, but of course I couldn't call him on it and tell him that he was full of shit.

He must have known I was disappointed because he reached over, took my hand, and raised it to his lips. "Hey, let's do something special tomorrow night instead. Just the two of us, okay?"

It wasn't prom, but it was better than nothing. It would be fun, maybe. It had been so long since we'd gone on a real date. "Really, just me and you?"

"Yeah," he said, smiling at me just like he used to. He really could be sweet when he wanted, and that smile never failed to convince me of just about anything.

"That sounds perfect," I told him, and then leaned over to kiss him on the cheek. That kiss led to a few more, and before I knew it, Marcus had passed up my house and was driving straight to his. He must have known that his parents weren't home, because as soon as we got out of the car, he was kissing me again. He barely had the front door open before he picked me up and carried me upstairs to his room. This was the Marcus I missed so much, the playful, intoxicating guy that I fell for two years ago. *My* Marcus.

We spent the rest of the evening wrapped in each other's arms, and when it was time for me to go home, I didn't want to. For the first time in a long while, I wanted to stay. Marcus walked me home, holding my hand the whole way, and right before we came into view of my front porch, Marcus tugged me behind a tree to kiss me once more.

"What time are you going to pick me up tomorrow?" I asked as we walked up the stairs to my porch.

"Be ready by seven," he said, and started to walk away.

I grabbed his hand and pulled him to me. "I can't wait," I whispered in his ear, which made him smile. Then he kissed me quickly and headed back home.

*****

I could hardly contain my excitement all day as I prepared for my date with Marcus. I did all the typical girly things that girls do before a hot date. I searched my entire closet until I found the perfect outfit for whatever he had planned, took a long, hot shower, gave myself a mani-pedi, shaved and tweezed; the works. When six o'clock finally rolled around, I spent a good thirty minutes putting on just the right amount of makeup, and after I got dressed, I stood back and gave myself the once-over in the mirror before slipping the necklace with Marcus's alpha ring hanging from it around my neck. By 6:55, I was ready and waiting.

At 7:15, I went back into my room and retouched my lip gloss. By the time the clock struck 7:30, the bad feeling I'd been ignoring since around 7:05 reared its ugly head, and by 7:45 I was officially pissed off. When the phone rang and I heard Marcus on the line, I knew exactly what he would say before he said it.

"Lily, I have to cancel tonight."

"Is everything okay?" I tried to mask the anger and disappointment in my voice.

"Something just came up. I'll call you tomorrow."

"Why don't you come by when you can?" I tried.

"Lily, I can't. Don't make this a big deal. I'll see you tomorrow. I gotta go."

Long after the line went dead, I stood in the kitchen with the phone in my hand. I couldn't even begin to wrap my head around all the emotions coursing through me. I was so mad I wanted to hit him, but at the same time tears threatened to fall as rejection and hurt tried to take the top spot. In the end, helplessness won out. Somehow, I was just supposed to accept how he treated me. I couldn't break up with him, and apparently he wasn't going to break up with me or he would have by now.

Immensely glad my mother wasn't here to witness it, I dragged myself to my room and took another shower, needing to wash away my perfect makeup and the sickening feeling of being trapped in a dysfunctional relationship. I threw on some old sweats and put Marcus's ring away before curling up on my bed. It was only then that I allowed my tears to spill down my face.

Chapter 2

Once the tears began, there was no stopping them. I turned over in my bed and clinched my eyes shut in hopes of blocking out the pain, but instead my mind drifted back to a time when things were different between Marcus and me. It was a happy time, which only caused my already battered heart to ache more. The memory, though a bit faded, replayed through my mind, and no matter how hard I tried I couldn't stop it from invading my brain.

It was almost two years ago when Marcus really noticed me. He'd been away most of the summer with his grandparents, and to celebrate his return his parents threw him an extravagant welcome-home party. The lodge was transformed into a breathtaking ballroom, and the entire pack eagerly awaited what was to be a black-tie affair. My mother bought me a beautiful, full-length, red dress that hugged my every curve, and I could hardly believe she would allow me to wear such a thing. But nobody told my mother no, so even though I felt completely self-conscious I put on the dress without question.

It wasn't long after we arrived that Marcus, looking excruciatingly gorgeous, made his entrance. The pack gathered around to greet him as if he were royalty. Unable to control my reaction, I rolled my eyes. But when I returned my attention to the prince of Red Ridge, his eyes were locked on me with such intensity that it caused my breath to hitch in my throat.

Marcus made his way through the crowd, shaking hands and kissing cheeks along the way, and then he stopped directly in front of me. He leaned close to whisper in my ear. "Was that eye-roll meant for me, Lily? And here I'd hoped you'd be happy I was home."

His breath tickled its way across my earlobe and neck, and then into my hair, forcing every nerve in my body to spring to life, and as his intoxicating scent washed over me, I involuntarily shivered. Immediately my cheeks flushed, and a wicked grin spread across his face.

"I enjoyed that reaction much better," he teased, and then he walked away before I could respond.

Silently, I ordered myself to get a grip. I'd known Marcus all my life and shouldn't come unraveled simply because he chose to acknowledge me for five seconds. But his attention didn't last for only five seconds, and I was definitely coming unraveled…completely. Marcus kept his eyes trained on me throughout dinner, and I couldn't help but ask myself, *why me?* He'd never paid much attention before, and I'd always kind of felt like an outsider, like I didn't really fit in. Even though my father was the pack's enforcer, my grandparents were elders, and I had plenty of friends…I don't know. I couldn't explain it. It wasn't really them; it was me.

The flirty glances soon turned to intense stares, and when he made his way over to ask me to dance, I had a feeling nothing would ever be the same between us. As he pulled me into his arms for the first time, heat spread through my body like a wildfire. He wrapped his arm around my lower back, dragging me even closer, as his lips neared my ear once again.

"God, Lily. You've never looked more beautiful. You don't know what you do to me in that dress."

His body stiffened as his gaze dipped down to my cleavage, and I found myself wondering if he could see my heart pounding in my chest. When his eyes found mine again, I teased, "Glad you're enjoying the view."

His eyes darkened as they ran the length of my body and back up again. "Oh, I'm more than enjoying it. In fact…" He didn't finish his thought. Instead, he led me off the dance floor and into the hallway. Barely out of view of the party, he pressed me up against the wall, and before my brain had time to register what was happening, his lips collided with mine. Hurried and full of need, we drank each other in, kissing until we were both out of breath.

With hooded eyes, Marcus ran his thumb down my cheek, and then he wrapped his hand behind my neck. "I want you, Lily. I want you to be mine." Gently guiding my lips back to his, he sealed his confession with another passionate kiss, and I knew right then I belonged to Marcus Walker.

From that night on we were inseparable. Every available second of every day was filled with Marcus, and within a month, he had me in his bed and had officially claimed me as his own. I was more than happy to consent, as I'd never been able to deny him anything. We were the perfect couple, too, totally and utterly in love.

By the time we were both eighteen, his parents affirmed that I would make the perfect mate for their future alpha. Once the words were spoken I knew there was no turning back, not that I had any intention of doing so. Not at that point. In fact, I'd never been more thrilled. The night that Marcus offered me his alpha ring was the best moment of my life, as it officially marked the beginning of our life together. We would be together forever, and I would one day be the alpha's wife.

Almost overnight everything began to fall apart. Slowly. The spark in his eyes when he looked at me began to fade, and somewhere along the way sex became something we did purely out of habit instead of desire. And as the passion fizzled, so did everything else. The fun and laughter in our relationship dissipated, and we no longer went out on dates or even hung out much with our friends in the pack.

I still loved him and wanted to rekindle what we once had, but whatever we used to be was dying, and as much as I wanted to deny it, we were on life-support and barely hanging on. Six months ago, on New Year's Day, I'd finally come to terms with the fact that what we'd once had was gone. Everything was over. But when I finally found the courage to break up with him, his eyes grew wide in shock and he did the very last thing I expected. He scooped me up in his arms and hugged me tightly. To this day, I'll never forget the words that came out of his mouth.

"You can't leave me, Lily." He was practically begging. "Please don't do this. I need you. I love you. We can make this work. I promise. Say you won't give up on us. Promise me." In all our time together he'd never spoken that way. Never had he seemed so vulnerable, so lost.

I pulled away to ask, "Do you really still love me?"

He answered with a deep, hard kiss and then pulled me down into his bed, tearing at my clothes as if desperate to be inside me at once. For the first time in a long while we made love like we used to, and afterward a tear fell down my face as I silently prayed that things would really be different from then on.

Of course, they weren't. That had been six months ago. Now, here he'd promised that we'd do something instead of prom and then ditched me when "something came up." I'm sure my mother would say he was taking care of business, too. In that moment I realized what it truly meant to be promised to the future alpha of the Red Ridge Pack. Marcus wouldn't let me go without a fight, but he also wasn't trustworthy. And my decisions were no longer my own.

Chapter 3

I woke up with puffy eyes and a hurt still lingering in my chest. The last thing I wanted to do was to put on a happy face first thing in the morning and go to our weekly pack meeting, but yet again, I had no choice in the matter. It was days like this when I wished I was human and could fake a stomachache to get out of it. I wasn't ready to face Marcus after last night, but avoiding him wouldn't work either, so I needed to slap on a smile and fake my way through it.

Of course, it was just my luck that Marcus was the very first person I saw when I walked into the lodge with my parents. I was raised not to make a scene, so when he walked up and greeted us, I was perfectly polite, even though it nearly killed me. My mother gushed over how handsome Marcus looked and how lucky I was that he'd picked me over all the other females in our pack. I resisted the urge to scream at her, to tell her just how lucky I felt last night when I was dismissed like a piece of garbage, and almost begged my father to get me the hell out of there; but I managed to keep my mouth shut. Marcus responded with a kind smile and then took my arm to lead me to our seats.

My silence got his attention, and he leaned in to ask me if I was okay.

Really?

"No, Marcus, everything is not okay. Why would it be okay?"

"Lily, you're being ridiculous."

I took his hand and marched him into the hallway, away from prying ears. "You knew how much I was looking forward to going somewhere and actually doing something fun with you last night." Marcus let his hand drop from mine. "I thought after Friday night that we were finally in a good place again. I'm just disappointed," I admitted, dropping my gaze to the floor and crossing my arms over my chest.

He lifted my head by placing his finger under my chin, and his eyes bored into mine. His stone-cold glare shot chills down my back. "Maybe it's time you get used to the disappointment," he stated flatly, then walked away.

He'd left me standing in the very same place that our relationship began two years ago. Leaning against the wall for support, I took several deep breaths, trying to fight back the tears that filled my eyes. But I wasn't sad. I was angry, so angry that I wasn't sure I could resist the desire to punch Marcus square in the nose, so before I headed back to my seat I took a much needed moment to collect myself.

When I returned, Marcus had moved to one of the chairs next to the alpha's podium. I made my way over to sit with my parents, but the longer I sat there, the more livid I became. My entire body was fuming, and I couldn't focus on anything except the rage rolling through me. As hard as I tried to avoid looking at Marcus, I couldn't. His mere presence was the spark that ignited my temper, and the sight of him was the only thing that kept me from breaking down in tears about this whole screwed-up situation.

Then I noticed something different about him. He looked almost…happy. Instead of stealing glances at me like he used to, his attention was elsewhere, focused on something behind me.

Trying not to be too obvious, I turned to see what had caught his interest. Noel, a girl a year older than us, was staring at Marcus like a lovesick puppy, and she wasn't even attempting to hide it.

Suddenly it all started to make sense. Was the bastard actually cheating on me with Noel? He had to be. That was why he'd been so distant, why he ditched me last night. The realization of it all was almost comical, and I literally had to cover my mouth to stop from laughing out loud. As soon as my smile was hidden, another thought occurred to me, causing all the anger to drain from my body. I was left numb, feeling nothing at all.

How can I be laughing when my boyfriend of two years is cheating on me? Oh my God, I don't love Marcus. Holy shit! He's cheating on me, and I don't feel anything.

Out of nowhere, the entire pack began clapping and cheering. I looked up just in time to see Marcus and his father walking toward me. Panicked, I turned to my mother, and she radiated pride. Marcus reached out his arm.

I took it automatically, just as he expected. Together we walked to the center of the stage as his father announced, "Ladies and gentleman, the future Mrs. Marcus Walker."

Marcus slipped a ring on my shaking finger, and just like that Marcus and I were officially engaged. Worst timing ever. My heart stopped, and I could hardly breathe. This couldn't be happening. No warning, no signs, no romantic proposal. Now I'd be married. I was trapped.

Fury filled me. The idea that Marcus and I were now engaged was completely absurd, especially now that I had suspicions about Noel. Standing in front of my entire pack, I felt like the biggest fraud. I couldn't stop myself from making eye contact with Noel, but as soon as her eyes connected with mine she looked down at her hands. She looked as miserable as I felt, and I almost felt sorry for her. Almost. We were the perfect pair, Noel and I. Two helpless girls caught up in a pack of lies.

"Fellow pack members, I cannot express how happy we are that our son has chosen Lily Michaels for his mate. Our families have always been close, and I have every confidence that she will make my son a happy man for the rest of his life," Marcus's father said as he wrapped his arm around my shoulder to give me a quick hug. "It's been a while since we've had a wedding here on the estate, and even longer since we've celebrated the passing of leadership from father to son. In just a few short weeks my son will replace me as alpha, and I could not be more proud. We will have a ceremony in his honor followed by an opulent dinner. And the first weekend in August, we will have the most beautiful wedding right here on the estate."

August? I looked at Marcus for the first time since this big announcement.

He didn't look shocked or surprised. He *knew* about this. Standing there holding my hand, he knew that his father was going to announce this and didn't tell me. Not only didn't he warn me, he didn't even bother to ask me if I wanted to marry him. I could feel the steam building inside. My free hand trembled as I boiled with rage, and I knew that my other hand, the one Marcus held, must have been trembling as well. My anger intensified as I thought about how this *should* have happened. All girls dream, or at least imagine, how their boyfriends would propose. Would they get down on one knee? Maybe fill the house with flowers? Make some type of grand gesture, or at least ask after an extravagant dinner at some beautiful restaurant. I'd never thought Marcus was capable of being *this* much of an inconsiderate ass.

"Smile, Lily. Everyone is staring," Marcus whispered and squeezed my hand in warning.

He was standing there smiling like this was the biggest and best day of his life. But then again, why wouldn't he be smiling? He had me for Friday nights, Noel for Saturdays, and soon he was going to be the alpha of the largest werewolf pack in New Mexico.

Chapter 4

It wasn't long before the lodge began to clear out. Marcus must have decided a long time ago that I was a complete pushover, but if he thought I was just going to let this pass without saying a word, he was dead wrong. I patiently watched as he stood near the exit chatting with Phillip, and waited for a sign that their conversation was coming to an end. As soon as the two of them shook hands, I marched over and grabbed Marcus by the arm.

Leading him toward the hallway where he'd so crudely informed me that I needed to get used to disappointment, I snapped, "We need to talk."

Marcus came to an abrupt halt, causing me to lose my grip on his arm and tumble forward a bit. "Slow down, Lily. If you want to talk, we aren't doing it here. Let's go back to my house. My parents are heading over to Phillip's to discuss his transition to enforcer."

Without waiting, I headed for the exit and called over my shoulder, "Fine. Let's go."

Neither of us spoke until his front door was locked behind us. He sat on the couch, but I had too much adrenaline coursing through me to do anything other than pace back and forth across the living room.

Marcus crossed his leg over his knee and threw his arm over the back of the couch. "Look, I know you're surprised."

Throwing my hands in the air I shouted, "Surprised? I'm a little more than surprised, Marcus. Did it even occur to you that you should *ask* me to marry you? What the hell was that? Because it certainly wasn't a proposal."

He sighed loudly. "Just calm down, Lily. You're making a bid deal out of nothing."

In mid-step, I stopped pacing as his words tore through me. "Not a big deal? You can't be serious! Because I think marriage is kind of a big deal, and last time I checked, you're supposed to ask a girl to marry you before you announce to the world that you're engaged."

Crossing his arms over his chest, he stated matter-of-factly, "It's not like you would have said no."

Rage engulfed me, swallowed me whole, and I could hardly see straight. As I fought back the urge to shift into wolf form and rip his throat out, I suddenly understood how someone could be capable of murder. I could totally relate to all those women in prison serving time for killing their man. Marcus was lucky that I regained control, because the words that had just come out of his mouth could have very well been his last.

My eyes narrowed as I glared at the cocky son-of-a-bitch who sat before me. "For your information, I would not have just said no. I would have said No-Fucking-Way! Especially since I finally opened my eyes and realized that you've been cheating on me with Noel Branson!"

Apparently, that got his attention. He shot to his feet and shouted, "Noel? You think I'm sleeping with Noel?"

"I don't just think, Marcus. I'm pretty damn sure of it. She was practically drooling over you all through the meeting, and the look on her face after your father's little announcement all but confirmed it. I guess you forgot to tell her about the engagement, too."

His cheeks flamed red as he grabbed me by the arms and forced me to look at him. "I-Am-Not-Cheating-On-You! Do you hear me? Not with Noel, not with anyone! I mean it, Lily."

I tried to pull away, but it only caused him to tighten his grip.

His fingers bit into my arms as I shouted, "Let. Me. Go!"

He released me, and I stumbled back a few steps, but I wasn't through just yet. "I know something is going on with her. You're really going to act like it's a coincidence that you've barely given me the time of day lately, and I just watched you two practically undressing each other with your eyes for the last hour. Really? What kind of fool do you think I am?"

Marcus took a step forward, but he stopped as soon as I took a step away. His face drained of color, and his eyes shifted to the floor. "Look, I'm sorry I grabbed your arms. I would never hurt you."

Hearing those words made sorrow replace my rage. "It's too late for that. You already have."

"You have to believe me. I'm not cheating on you. Noel has always had a crush on me, but it doesn't matter. There is nothing going on, and there is never going to be."

I looked down at the ring on my finger. Even I couldn't pretend that it wasn't absolutely breathtaking. The center held a flawless princess-cut rock, and tons of tiny diamonds surrounded it and lined the white-gold band. It was perfect, but that didn't mean that it belonged on my hand. I held it out in front of me. "What about this?"

"What do you mean, 'what about this'?" He looked confused.

"I don't know what I mean. All I know is that everything seems so messed up."

"I know. But every couple goes through tough times, right? It will get better. Just give it time."

I nodded my head but had a horrible feeling that all the time in the world wouldn't be able to save us.

Chapter 5

The end of high school came and went, and finally it was the first week of summer, and not only was I finally a high school graduate but engaged to be married as well. Both situations somehow left me more lost than ever. While others were planning for college, I was stuck planning a wedding—a wedding I wasn't convinced should even be taking place.

To make matters worse, somebody must have decided along the way that I didn't need a college education. Who needs college when you're going to be the alpha's dutiful wife, one who sits by his side, plays the part and shoots out plenty of pups? I'd never imagined myself as a barefoot-and-pregnant kind of girl, yet here I stood imagining my new future. Sadly, it didn't look so bright.

Since the announcement of our engagement, Marcus had grown more distant than ever, and according to him I just needed to get used to it. How the hell had this happened? Why did he even want to marry me?

Obviously he was miserable, and most days I doubted he even loved me anymore—if he ever had. The only good thing I had to say about him was that he hadn't been sneaking off, so he had either stopped seeing Noel or was being extra careful.

Summer had always been my favorite time of year, yet for the last several days I'd taken to hanging out in my bedroom more and more, at times not bothering to get out of the tank top and gym shorts that I had worn to bed the night before. I just needed time to think. To figure out my next move. Could I really be forced to marry Marcus? What if I just said no? What then? Would my friends and family—?

Just as I began to consider the possibility of breaking things off for good with Marcus, I heard footsteps headed up the stairs. Mom was on her way to my room. There was no other reason to come up here besides to drag me back to civilization, so I mentally prepared myself for battle, ready to admit that Marcus and I were not meant to be. Ready to fight the battle that would be the worst I'd ever fought.

Instead, when I opened up to a knock, I was shocked to find my father standing in the doorway.

His sad eyes caused a lump to form in my throat. He felt sorry for me. It was written all over his face. He'd always been the one I went to for comfort, the one who somehow managed to make everything better. He might have been the enforcer of our pack, the big, tough guy who was the alpha's right-hand man, but with me he'd always been a big softy. More than ever I wanted to throw myself into his arms and beg him to help me get out of this mess, but the look on his face kept me from doing so.

He just stood there right outside my bedroom door, not saying a word.

"What are you doing up here, Dad?"

He swallowed, as if it pained him to say whatever he'd come up here to say. "I just wanted to check on you. You've been up here a lot lately. Maybe you should come down and eat something."

"I'm not hungry. What's this really about? You haven't been up to my room in forever." I cringed at the harshness in my voice, but I had a feeling my mother was behind his impromptu visit.

He shifted from foot to foot and blew out a deep breath before finally answering. "Look, Lillian. I know things are a little rocky with Marcus right now, but that's how relationships are sometimes. You need to find a way to work through it. You're going to be married soon, so, honey, you need to do what you can to make the best of it."

Make the best of it? Seriously? That's his advice? Unsure of what to say next, I backed up and sat down on my bed. Dad followed suit and took a seat next to me.

I shifted my body toward him and finally admitted out loud, "But what if I don't want to make it work, Dad?"

He wrapped his arm around me and rested his head on top of mine. "Don't say that, honey. You and Marcus are right for each other. You've just hit a rough patch. Give it some time and things will turn around. I'm sure of it. Promise me you'll try. Don't give up just yet."

I answered with a heavy sigh. If my father wasn't going to back me on this, no one would. But I wasn't going to just sit back and be forced into a loveless, hopeless marriage. For my father's sake, I would try. One last time. I did love Marcus once, and if we could find a way to get back to the place we used to be, this could work.

If not, I'd need a Plan B.

*****

That night I curled my hair, put on makeup and perfume, and dressed in my favorite cut-off shorts and a low-cut tank. After I slipped Marcus's necklace on, I hurried down the stairs and out the front door, thankful my parents were spending the evening at the Stantons'.

The entire way to Marcus's, I rehearsed exactly what I would say, and as I knocked on the door I plastered a smile on my face. His parents greeted me a little more excitedly than usual, and they sent me up to the game room to find their son.

He barely looked away from the television to tell me hello, so I sank down into the couch and pretended to watch a rerun of *The Real World* with him. At the commercial break, I turned my body toward him and set Plan A into action.

"So, I was thinking we haven't had a lot of time together lately, and since it's summer now, maybe we could get away for the weekend. Maybe a trip to the river?"

He huffed. *Huffed!* Leaning forward, he placed his elbows on his knees, and his eyes fell to the floor. "I don't think so, Lily. I have a lot going on here. I can't take off for the whole weekend."

I tried again. "Well, maybe just the day then? We can go hiking or something."

He sat back on the couch and finally looked my way. "Really, Lily? Hiking?"

"Okay, bad idea. Oh, I heard about a music festival in Red Ridge this weekend. We can go tonight. Come on, it will be fun." I tried to keep my voice upbeat, but this was harder than I thought, and he wasn't making it any easier.

Marcus stood and ran his fingers through his hair. Letting out another huff, he turned his back to me and said, "Yeah, I don't think so. Besides, I have some stuff to take care of tonight. I am in the process of learning how to run this pack, you know. I have responsibilities, not that you would know anything about that."

Instinctively I shot up from the couch. My blood was boiling, my ears ringing. He had some nerve talking to me about responsibility! I knew all too well about responsibility. This time it was me who huffed as I threw my hands up in frustration. "What's going on with us, Marcus? Is this what our lives are going to be like?

Barely talking, never doing anything together? We used to have so much fun together."

Marcus turned back to face me once more. His eyebrows furrowed, and he looked as frustrated as I felt. "Oh, please. Get over yourself. Poor Lillian Michaels, never gets to have any fun anymore. Do you even hear yourself right now?"

"What about you, Marcus? Do you hear *yourself*? You treat me like shit. Like you don't even love me anymore. I can't figure out why you're even marrying me."

Crossing his arms defensively, Marcus took a step in my direction, closing a bit of the distance between us. "Look, it is what it is. We are getting married. End of story. I feel just as stuck as you do, but you don't see me crying about it."

Stuck? *He* felt stuck? His words sliced right through me. My heart constricted and tears filled my eyes. I hated myself for crying, for doing exactly what he said I'd do, but I wasn't as weak as he thought. To prove it, I eliminated every last bit of space between us, looked straight into his eyes and asked the question I'd been dying to know the answer to. "Then why the hell are we getting married?"

Suddenly looking completely dejected, his shoulders slumped as he let his body fall to the couch. His head rested against the cushion behind him, and his eyes closed and remained that way as he spoke. "Because we have to."

Slowly he opened his eyes and lifted his head, but he avoided eye contact as he continued. "You aren't supposed to know this, so you better keep your mouth shut. Your parents were supposed to have a son. Their son would have become my enforcer, just as your father is my dad's enforcer. But they had you and then weren't able to have any more children. So our parents agreed—to keep your family in the alpha's circle—we would be married. Then your mom and dad wouldn't lose their status in the pack when Phillip became my enforcer. It's been their plan for years. When I fell for you, they couldn't have been happier. Everything was falling into place. I only found out when we started drifting apart. My dad told me the truth, told me I had to marry you. There's no going back now. Our marriage was arranged, and we have to go through with it."

My body dropped down on the couch next to him as the truth swallowed me whole. Everyone had been lying to me all this time. My parents, Marcus, his parents… It had all been one giant lie, an elaborate charade. I couldn't even find words to respond. Finally the ugly truth was revealed, but I couldn't believe it. I didn't want to believe it. My parents, the two people who were supposed to love me the most in this world, traded me, their only child, to keep their status in the pack.

My head was spinning and I wasn't sure if my legs would even cooperate, but I needed to get out of there. Needed to get away from all of them.

Without another word, I stood up and walked away. His parents said goodbye as I passed, but I just kept moving. I couldn't pretend right now.

Once outside, I rushed home, flew up the stairs, and threw myself down on my bed. After spending a half hour or so in a state of complete shock, I sat up and grabbed the phone without giving myself time to chicken out.

It rang twice before she picked up.

"Hey, Tiff, wanna get off the estate for a while? I need to get out of here."

Chapter 6

"Lily, freakin' relax! I swear if you pass out I will leave your ass in the car," Tiffany yelled from the driver's seat of her Pontiac Sunfire.

Leaving the estate had felt like the right thing to do at the time, but as we drove under the big sign advertising Red Ridge's First Ever Music Festival, I was having second thoughts. I'd never done anything like this before, never once gone against my parents' wishes, never broken a single rule. I couldn't stop thinking about what my mother would say if she knew her perfect little princess was here without Marcus.

Shit! *Marcus.* He'd kill me if he knew I'd run off with Tiffany of all people. And if I somehow survived Marcus's wrath, his father would probably put me under house arrest. Maybe he'd implant me with a tracking device like a damn dog. This was a very bad idea. I looked down at my trembling hands and almost begged Tiffany to take me back home.

Almost.

When I looked out the window at the lights in the distance, at the crowd of people filing in the front gates, I decided this was something I needed to do before I became Mrs. Marcus Walker. Then I closed my eyes and reminded myself for the hundredth time since we drove off the estate, *Who the hell cares what they'd say or do? For one night I'm going to do what I want.*

I took a deep breath and tried to relax. "Okay, I'm fine."

She glanced my way, laughed and shook her head. "Yeah, right."

She parked the car in the free gravel lot, checked her makeup, and was out of the car before I even had a chance to open my door. Tiffany stood there with her hands on her hips, waiting. When I finally got out, she hooked her arm through mine, and together we walked through the gates of the fairgrounds.

Before we did anything, I needed to make sure Tiffany understood what was at stake. I pulled her to a stop and made her look at me. "You have to promise me that you won't tell anyone that I came here tonight. I mean it, Tiff. If my parents or Marcus find out, it won't be pretty. Seriously."

Tiffany looked around before saying, "Listen, I turn eighteen at the end of summer, and then I'm gone. The estate will be in my rearview mirror before sundown on August twenty-third. I'm not sticking around for a single day longer than I have to. You keep my secret, and I'll keep yours. We take it to our graves."

I was absolutely stunned. I'd never heard of anyone voluntarily leaving our pack before. I didn't even realize that you could, that the pack would let you. I leaned in to ensure that no one else could hear. "Really? You're just going to take off? You aren't worried they'll come after you?"

"It's not likely. Once you leave, you're out. There's no going back, no second chances, but I've got some money saved. I don't plan on coming back. I'd rather be homeless."

I stared at her, wide-eyed and speechless. She linked her arm through mine once again and continued walking.

"Look, I swear I won't tell a soul that you did anything remotely fun tonight. Okay?" she said.

I nodded, but she didn't notice because she'd already set her sights on some guy passing by in the opposite direction. As soon as their eyes connected, she dropped my arm and started drifting toward him. "I'll see you later, Michaels. Meet me back right here in like an hour," she yelled over her shoulder as she raced to catch up with her pick for the night.

Un-freakin'-believable! I should have known Tiffany would ditch me for the first hot-looking human who looked her way. I surveyed the area but wasn't quite sure what to do with myself.

Standing alone in the middle of the festival with so much to see and do, I no longer felt nervous about the chance of getting caught. Instead I felt excited, almost giddy. I felt free for the first time in my life, and it was a heady feeling that scared the shit out of me, but only because I liked it so much. I knew I shouldn't be there, but I no longer cared and I refused to let fear rule my life, at least for one night.

Right then, amongst the crowd of strangers surrounding me, I made a silent vow to myself that I'd make the most of it. And I did. After my little internal pep talk I started walking up and down through the rows of booths that were set up with humans selling everything from sodas and hotdogs to airbrushed T-shirts and old album covers.

When I found my way back to the front entrance, Tiffany was nowhere to be seen. I bought myself a Coke and went to listen to the band that was setting up nearby at the main stage.

A small crowd already filled the area up front. Waiting for the band to start, I sat on a small wooden bench off to the side of the stage to hear what all the hype was about.

"Ladies and gentlemen," a man announced over the intercom, "please welcome to the main stage, all the way from Taos, THE SPASTIC BAMBIS!"

Their small following cheered as the guys came out on stage. Moments later, the intro to "When I Come Around" by Green Day blasted from the speakers. By the time they got to the chorus, more and more people stopped to crowd around.

They were good, but they were no Green Day. I didn't see what all the fuss was about until I got up and walked over to get a better look. Three very hot guys were spread out across the stage singing and playing their hearts out. Tiffany was going to be pissed she missed this.

As I walked around the back of the crowd to get to the other side, *he* came into view. I was totally mistaken; this band had three very hot guys *and one drop-dead gorgeous bass player*. Watching the tattoo-covered muscles of his arms move to the beat of the music as he played was hypnotic.

Without a second thought, I pushed my way toward the stage to get a closer look. He was tall and lean and absolutely stunning, a vision in black pants. Somehow, I managed to tear my eyes away from his arms long enough to look at the rest of him.

Good heavens, he didn't disappoint. He had that bad-boy-rock-star, I-don't-give-a-shit vibe, beginning with his black steel-toed Doc Martens, up past his snugly fit Sex Pistols T-shirt, all the way to his blond, spiky hair dyed blood-red at the tips. He looked nothing like the guys I was used to, and nothing like Marcus.

That was just fine by me.

I stood transfixed while his band played a few other songs. At the end of the fourth, he bent down to pick up some water, and I had never in my life been more jealous of something than I was of that bottle when it touched his lips. He might have been one of the most perfect creatures I'd ever had the luxury of seeing.

And then he started to sing. His voice…oh the gods…his voice. It was the kind of voice that was meant to whisper sweet nothings and dirty promises in the darkest hour of the night.

I sucked in a breath and stared, completely consumed. He stood perfectly still, his eyes closed, his guitar resting against his back, both hands gently holding the microphone while he sang the sexiest version of Radiohead's "Creep" that I had ever heard.

His eyes opened as he reached the first chorus, and even from as far back as I stood I could tell that they were a startling pale blue. For some reason his eyes reminded me of a swimming pool. Suddenly I was thinking of swimming. Then I was swimming with him. It was dark and we were naked, and…

Oh my God…he just caught me staring at him while daydreaming about him naked!

My face had to have been ten shades of red. I figured he might smile and look away, go back to singing all sexy-like with his eyes closed, but he didn't. He stared directly at me and I couldn't move, much less look away, not when he was watching me just as wantonly as I was watching him. When he finally did smile at me, I freaked.

Completely overcome with humiliation, I turned and took off toward my pathetic, safe little bench, out of view of the sexy musician. How embarrassing and completely cliché! I was the stupid, lonely teenage girl drooling over the bad-boy rocker with the sexy arms and the voice that could melt chocolate. There was probably at least twenty other girls standing there fantasizing about him too.

I stayed glued to my bench until the Spastic Bambis finished their set and another less-sexy band took the stage. Suddenly, the urge to get out of there was overwhelming. I needed to find Tiffany, drag her ass to the car, and bury myself under the covers when I got home.

The crowd was beginning to thin out, so I got up and started to make my way back to the main gate. I didn't get more than a few feet away before someone grabbed my arm. I turned around expecting to see Tiffany and her latest catch, but I had never been more wrong.

Chapter 7

My eyes shot open in shock at the sight of the ridiculously sexy guitar player holding my arm. His smile lit up his entire face, and I found myself in awe of the pure beauty of something as simple as a grin.

All too soon he let go of my arm, but steadily he held my gaze as he said, "Hey, I saw you out there in the crowd and couldn't let you run off before I introduced myself. I'm Paul. Paul Wright. And I promise I'm not crazy. 'Cause you're kinda lookin' at me like I might be a serial killer or something."

Shaking myself out of my starstruck haze, I managed to close my mouth and form some semblance of a smile. In my head, all I could think was *no freakin' way*, but after a second or two I managed to piece together a few coherent words as I popped my knuckles repeatedly.

"Uh, I'm Lillian." Not great, but at least it was something.

He stuck out his hand for me to shake. "Nice to meet you, Lillian…"

He was obviously waiting for me to continue, and for about a second I considered ending our conversation right there and walking away, but watching his pale-blue eyes dance with possibilities, I couldn't stop the words from tumbling out of my mouth. "Lillian Michaels. You were really great up there. You're *not* a serial killer, are you? Because if you are, I should probably just be on my way."

He laughed at my lame joke. I'd forgotten how good it felt to actually make someone laugh. With his hand still wrapped around mine he replied, "Definitely not a serial killer. Okay, here it is. Like I said, my name is Paul. I just graduated from college. I'm twenty-two. No girlfriend, no kids, no drugs. Never been arrested. And I've never been one to let an opportunity pass me by, and when I saw you, I just knew you were someone I had to meet."

Reluctantly I pulled my hand away. "So you think I'm an opportunity, huh?"

"That really didn't come out right, did it? What I meant to say was I couldn't pass up the opportunity to meet someone so beautiful. A girl who looks like she would be very hard to forget. You are aware that there is not another female here who could even compare, right?"

Never in my life had I been more intrigued, but I shot him a look that I hoped said that I thought he was full of shit.

Twisting the bands around his wrist, he let out a quiet chuckle. "You're not going to make this easy on me, are you, Lillian Michaels?"

I crossed my arms and shot my hip out to the side. "Well, I wouldn't want you thinkin' that I was just another *easy* opportunity," I teased, hoping my cheeks weren't as flushed as they felt.

I had no idea what had gotten into me. I was actually flirting with a bass player from a punk band who had bright red hair tips and tattoos covering his arms, but I couldn't seem to stop myself. His playful demeanor was contagious, and it had been entirely too long since I had any fun.

He put his hand over his heart, pretending to be in pain. "Come on, you're killing me here. Am I ever gonna dig myself out of this one? Because I'd really like the chance to try."

"Well, I hope you have a shovel because it looks like you might need it."

Taking a step in my direction, he ran his fingers down the length of my arm before scooping my hand back up in his. "I'll dig all night as long as you promise to stick around."

My pulse quickened as my entire body flooded with warmth, and suddenly I realized just how much trouble this guy could be. I didn't even know him. He could be a total sleazeball on the hunt for some random girl to lure back to his van. Besides that, Marcus would kill me for even stopping to talk to this guy—after he killed the poor human first.

Before I could change my mind, I pulled my hand out of Paul's grasp and said, "You know, I really need to find my friend, but it was nice meeting you. Have a good night, Paul." I turned, forcing one foot in front of the other and didn't look back.

I'd made it about five feet before I noticed that I wasn't alone. Falling into step, Paul flashed me a crooked grin and shrugged his shoulders. "No worries. I'll help you find her. It would be my pleasure. Wait...your friend. She is a girl, right?"

"You know, that was supposed to be your cue to move along."

He slightly tilted his head to the side and playfully nudged me with his elbow. "Well, I've never been real good with cues. Just ask the lead singer in my band."

"I see. That explains a lot actually. And yes, for the record, my friend is a girl. Not that it matters," I teased as I continued walking and scanning the crowd in search of my domestic-loving partner in crime.

Paul followed alongside, his hands shoved deep in his pockets, and he looked around as if he would actually be able to spot a girl that he'd never seen.

"What exactly are you looking for?" I asked, popping my knuckles yet again.

"Your friend, of course. And maybe some funnel cake." As if on cue, a funnel cake stand came into view, and he tilted his head in its direction. "See, it's meant to be. How 'bout it? Want to share one? My treat."

"Well, if it's meant to be, I guess I can't say no, now can I? But I should warn you. I can do some serious damage to a funnel cake."

He pulled his hand out of his pocket, grabbed mine, and pulled me in the direction of the stand. "Oh yeah? Prove it."

Hand in hand, we stood in line for the deep-fried dessert, and for some reason that I couldn't explain, I didn't pull my hand away this time. Instead, I let myself enjoy the odd connection we seemed to share. I just hoped Tiffany didn't decide to show back up and catch me red-handed. I wasn't sure I could explain since I didn't really understand it myself.

Just as promised, Paul treated me to a funnel cake, and we headed over to a patch of grass so we could sit down and enjoy the powdered sugar–covered monstrosity. After a few failed attempts with a plastic fork, we both set utensils aside and dug in with our fingers. It only took a few minutes to devour the entire thing, and once the plate was empty we laughed about the mess we had managed to make.

I held both hands up and said, "I think we're going to need some napkins."

"Napkins? We don't need no stinkin' napkins. Betcha I can lick mine clean before you can."

"You're on," I countered, and without warning I began quickly licking away the sugary mess from my fingers.

With his eyes glued to mine, Paul did the same, and I couldn't help but laugh at how silly he looked. I couldn't remember the last time I'd had so much fun. Had I ever? I'd always been so worried about what everyone else thought of me. As the enforcer's daughter and then the future alpha's girlfriend I'd never really gotten to just be me, and it kind of broke my heart to think that I might never get to feel this way again.

Seconds later, he shouted, "Done!" and raised his hands in victory.

With several fingers still to go, I shrugged and said, "I guess that means you win."

"So what's my prize?"

"Prize? Who said anything about a prize?"

He picked up the empty plate, stood, and then held out his hand to help me up. Once I was on my feet and standing directly in front of him, he stepped toward me and said, "There has to be a prize. It's like a rule. Every contest needs a prize."

I watched him lick the last bit of sugar off his lips, and butterflies stirred in my stomach as I imagined what it would feel like to push up on my tiptoes and close the last bit of space between us. With his lips only a breath away, I'd never felt more drawn to anyone in my life. I wanted to taste him, to have his lips collide with mine and kiss me until we were gasping for air.

"Well?" The sound of his voice interrupted my fantasy.

"Well what?" I asked, trying desperately to still my racing heart.

"My prize? How about your phone number?"

Shit! So not an option. I glanced down at my watch and looked around at the thinning crowd. "You know, we should probably go wash our hands, and then I really need to find Tiffany."

He let me change the subject without question, and I was filled with relief…at first. But as I washed my hands in the restroom and glanced up into the mirror, regret crept its way into my heart. What if I never saw him again? It would be for the best, and in my mind, I knew that, but my heart constricted at the thought of this guy walking out of my world forever.

I left the restroom knowing that this night would soon end, but I smiled through my sadness when Paul wrapped his arm around my waist. "Where to, Lillian Michaels?"

We searched the entire fairgrounds, but Tiffany was nowhere in sight and I began to wonder if she had left me there. "I think I'll just wait by the front gate. I'm sure she will show up soon."

He checked his watch and said, "It's almost closing time. Come on, I'll wait with you. If she doesn't show, I'll give you a ride home."

As we headed toward the gate, I racked my brain for any viable excuse to take a cab. There was no way I could let him take me home. I could only pray that Tiffany wouldn't leave me stranded in Red Ridge with no way home.

We sat down against the entrance gate, and it wasn't long before a very angry Tiffany was heading our way. Her eyes landed on Paul. She took a moment to give him an appraising look before she turned to me and ranted, "Where the hell have you been? I've been looking for you for like an hour."

At the same time, Paul and I stood up and dusted off our clothes.

"I've been looking for you too. Where did you run off to earlier?"

She let out a disgusted sigh. "Don't ask. This night was a total bust. Let's get out of here."

My gut twisted at the thought of saying goodbye to Paul. "Hey, I'll meet you at the car. Okay, Tiff?"

Her attention shifted between Paul and me, and with a knowing nod she made her way through the parking lot.

I just stood there speechless. My heart constricted at the thought of never seeing him again. He was practically a stranger, but I wanted to latch on to Paul Wright and never let go because it killed me to think that when I walked away tonight, this perfect guy who made me feel smart and funny and beautiful, and *wanted*, would be nothing more than a memory.

I watched as Paul grabbed a flyer off the gate. He turned it over, pulled out a Sharpie from his pocket and scribbled something across the page. Then he folded up the paper and said, "If you won't give me yours, at least you'll have mine. You know, just in case you want to call. That can be my prize."

As I took the paper, our hands touched and he gently pulled me toward him. Every cell in my body was begging him to kiss me, but I was simultaneously struck with panic at the thought that he might.

His lips almost touched mine before he whispered, "Good night, Lillian Michaels." Then he turned around and left me standing there, watching him as he walked out of my life.

It kind of felt like he took a little piece of me with him, leaving behind a hole inside that would forever remain empty because I'd never know what might have been.

Chapter 8

My fantastically chaotic dream filled with random visions of swimming pools, guitars, and funnel cakes ended with Marcus's surprise appearance. How Marcus ended up there I had no idea, but his face in the midst of the festival shot me out of my bed and filled me with nervous energy.

I wanted to crawl back into bed and get a few more hours sleep before I was forced to get ready for Marcus's ceremony, but I knew my body wouldn't allow it. I slipped on my flip-flops, stopped by the bathroom, and snuck my way downstairs to the backdoor.

I unlocked the mudroom door and propped it slightly open before stripping down and taking wolf form. This is what I needed to burn off some energy, a good, long run. I took off out my backdoor and ran as fast as my four legs would go down the road to the lake. Only then did I slow my pace. The lake was one of my favorite places to think, but today I didn't want to think. I just wanted to feel.

I stretched my legs, my back, my neck, and shook out my fur before sitting back and taking a deep breath of the clean morning air. Once my lungs were full, and my body felt awake, I took off on my usual route.

I tried to clear my mind of all my troubles: Marcus, the wedding, my attraction to Paul, everything. I focused on the slight burn in my muscles and the sights and sounds of the forest around me. Oddly enough, it was only in times like this that I really felt like a werewolf. I'd never admit it out loud, mostly because my perfect werewolf mother would kill me, but I'd always felt more human than wolf. I couldn't explain it. I'd just always felt different, but it wasn't like I could talk to anyone about it. They'd think I was insane, and I was starting to think that they would probably be right. Why else would I be lusting after a hot human bass player in a punk band?

By the time I made it back home, I was feeling much better. The itchy, nervous feeling under my skin had subsided, and I was able to relax in a hot bath. I took my time getting ready for the ceremony, knowing that I needed to look my best since all eyes were going to be on the "happy couple."

When I emerged from my bathroom, I saw that my mom had laid out a few dress choices for today. I was surprised that she even gave me options and didn't just pick one out for me. After careful consideration, I decided on the simple, light-blue sheath dress and black strappy sandals. I put my hair up, leaving just a few strands down by my face, and then stood back to look at myself in the mirror. Who I saw didn't feel much like me, but she did look like the perfect alpha's wife.

Damn, Mom is scary good.

This was the first alpha ceremony that I had ever been to, so I didn't have anything to compare it with, but in my opinion it was a bit over the top. All the important families had a role, and I soon learned that my duty was to stand by Marcus but noticeably off to the side. Of course, my role didn't require me to say anything.

After the official ceremony there was a dinner and some dancing. Marcus, always the showman, turned on the charm and worked the room in true alpha form. He even had *me* fooled for a second. If only he were like that all the time, maybe I wouldn't be dreading August so much.

I watched as Marcus danced with several girls from his pack—not once with Noel, I might add. Then Marcus and I sat alone at a table in the front of the room, and every time someone would come to congratulate him, he would place his hand on mine, just long enough for them to notice.

Finally, the party ended and it was time to leave. I was dead on my feet from smiling brightly and pretending to be perfect. But just as I was telling the Walkers what a fabulous ceremony it was, Mrs. Walker cut in and said, "No dear, you can't go yet. We have a surprise for you. An early wedding gift, if you will."

I looked over to Marcus, and he just shrugged. I didn't know why I even bothered looking to him for answers. He wouldn't give them to me anyway.

My parents said their goodbyes, and I could tell by the way my mom hesitated she was hoping for an invitation to witness the big gift, but it didn't come. Marcus, his parents and I left the lodge and got into Mr. Walker's car. Marcus didn't say a word as we drove the short distance to the end of the lake. When the car stopped, we all got out and stood in the driveway of one of the most beautiful homes on the estate.

"For you both," Mr. Walker said, giving us each a key to the house.

A house? They're giving us a house?

My anxiety rose to an all-time high, and I didn't know what to say. It would make a breathtaking home, huge, grand, absolutely gorgeous. But it felt more like a cage, and I'd be its prisoner, trapped inside, for better or worse, living a life that I didn't want with a man who didn't want me.

"We are so happy for you. We want your married life to start in this beautiful home," Mrs. Walker said, coming to stand by me. "I cannot wait until that house is filled with my rambunctious grandkids."

Grandkids? Holy Mother of God! Grandkids?

"It's amazing. Thank you," I said, finally finding the words, but my voice cracked and it felt like any minute my legs were going to give out. A full-on panic attack just might be on the horizon, especially if Mrs. Walker mentioned babies again.

"You two go on in. I hope you don't mind that I went ahead and furnished a few of the rooms for you," Mrs. Walker added.

"Of course we don't mind, Mom," Marcus said.

Mr. Walker ushered us to the door and told us to take our time and look around. They left us there alone to face our soon-to-be reality.

Marcus, without a word, opened the front door and stepped aside to let me walk in first. The house was truly beautiful: high ceilings, beautiful furniture; even a picture of the two of us taken over the holidays was framed and hung on the wall.

I set my key on the table in the entryway and walked down the hall. I opened one of the doors to find what was to be our bedroom, and I wanted to cry. It was stunning. It deserved to belong to a couple that truly loved each other.

I turned to leave but Marcus blocked my way. I could see it in his eyes that he was feeling the same way, but I knew by now he would never admit to it. I walked around him and up the stairs to find another room completely furnished.

Seeing this room stole my breath away and filled my eyes with tears. His mother had completely decorated and furnished a nursery. It was all too much. Finding out that our relationship was basically set up, that our marriage was arranged, that Marcus didn't love me, knowing now that I didn't love him was just too much. I sat on the floor and sobs wracked me. This was my life. I was going to marry

Marcus. I was going to have his children. I would never truly love a man, and one would never really love me.

"Over the top, right?" Marcus said, kneeling before me. I looked at him through my tears and forced myself up off the floor. We were both stuck, trapped in this impossible situation. I wanted to tell him that he deserved to be happy, that *I* deserved to be happy, but that conversation was played out. It would only end with us fighting anyway, so what was the point? Instead, I turned and walked away.

I was mentally and emotionally exhausted by the time I got home and planned to shut myself away in my room, but of course Mom stayed up to hear all the details.

"So, what was the big surprise?" she asked as soon as I walked in.

I put my purse down and counted to ten before I tuned in to my giddy-schoolgirl act, turned to my mother and gushed, "Oh my God, Mom! It's a house! The biggest on the estate. You and Dad just have to go see it tomorrow. I'm going to run upstairs right now and call Mrs. Walker to thank her again. I can't believe it! 'Night, Mom!" Then I took off like a bat out of hell before she saw through my façade.

"Oh, that's fabulous, honey! I can't wait to go see your new house," my mom called out as I ran up the stairs to my room.

As I lay on my bed, my thoughts surprisingly weren't on the horrible day I had just experienced. Instead I was thinking about eyes the color of swimming pools, a voice that caused my insides to quiver, and the folded piece of paper with a telephone number on it in my drawer.

I'd only had one real boyfriend in my life, but I wasn't a complete idiot when it came to the rules of dating. I knew it was too soon to call him. Still, that didn't stop me from reaching for his number. I stared at the messy script on the neon-green slip of paper. I held on to that paper, folding and unfolding it, setting it down and picking it back up, until I decided that I was nowhere near cool enough to wait.

My hands clenched the paper so tightly that my knuckles were white as I considered what this one decision could set in motion. I ignored all the rational parts of my brain warning me not to do this. For once in my life, I needed to do something just for me. Something crazy. Something completely irrational.

I picked up my phone, held my breath, and dialed his number.

Chapter 9

Turning into the parking lot of a trendy little store called Tower Records in Taos, I tried to convince myself that this wasn't such a bad idea, but when I pulled down the visor to check my makeup in the mirror, I couldn't deny the fact that I looked guilty as hell. Just a couple of hours ago I was standing in the house that I would soon share with my future husband. So, on what planet would sneaking off to meet another guy constitute a good idea?

I shut the visor and just sat there in my car staring out the windshield. Was I really going to do this? Just walk on in and pretend I was an ordinary girl who wasn't just a werewolf but an engaged werewolf, there to meet a guy, and a human guy no less? I couldn't explain, even to myself, why I wanted to do this. It was like there was this voice inside me telling me that if I didn't I would regret it for the rest of my life. I needed to get out of this car and walk into that goddamned record store.

This had to be the dumbest idea I've ever had, but it was exactly what I was going to do.

My heart pounded in my chest at the mere thought of seeing the gorgeous bass player again. If I didn't get out of the car soon, I was going to lose my nerve and end up driving back to the estate full of regret and what-ifs. Reminding myself that you only live once, I opened my car door, got out, and rushed up to the entrance before I could talk myself out of it. Hopefully, guilt would be easier to swallow than regret.

When I walked in, I was greeted by a guy who looked like he'd fit right in with the stoner crew from Red Ridge High. With sleepy eyes and a goofy grin, he glanced up from his post at the front counter and said, "Hey, what's up? Lemme know if ya need somethin'."

I scanned the aisles separated with rows and rows of CDs but didn't see any sign of the punk-rocker from the music-fest, and he was pretty hard to miss. Unsure of what to do with myself, I sifted through the CDs nearest me, but since country music wasn't really my thing I decided to search around for something more my taste.

As I found the R&B section, my eyes landed on the backside of a guy wearing headphones who was shelving old cassette tapes in the back corner of the store. His hair was blond, spiked up with plenty of gel, and he wore a flannel shirt, tattered jeans, and combat boots. I watched for a while as he bobbed his head to the music in his ears, but he must have felt me staring because out of nowhere he put the cassettes down and turned around.

The blood-red tips of his hair were gone, but he looked every bit like the rock star who knocked me off my feet almost twenty-four hours before. His flannel shirt hung unbuttoned over a plain white T-shirt, and the sleeves were rolled up just a bit, enough to see his tattoos peeking out and the multiple bands tied around his wrists. Two thick silver chains hung from a side belt loop that swooped down and connected to the back pocket of his loosely fitted, worn-out jeans.

His look screamed, *I'm too cool for my own damn good, definitely too cool for you,* but when his eyes met mine and a stunning smile broke out across his equally stunning face, I couldn't stop my feet from moving in his direction.

I was drawn to him like a moth to a flame, and the notion that this might have been a bad idea flew right out the window.

He met me halfway and said, "Hey, Lillian Michaels. I was hoping you'd show up. I was afraid you'd change your mind."

How could he possibly know that? I stared up at him incredulously. "Why would I change my mind?"

He shrugged his shoulders and then laced his fingers through mine as he pulled me toward the back room. "I don't know. You just seemed…unconvinced. But I have big plans to change that. I just need to clock-out real quick. Then I can get started."

"Get started on what?"

He stopped in front of the door that said Employees Only and replied, "Convincing you, of course."

Just the thought of what those four little words could mean stirred something inside me that I didn't even know existed, and if I had dropped dead right there in that moment, I would have died a very happy lady.

We walked a few blocks from the record store and arrived at a huge open area full of outdoor shops, art displays, food carts, and street performers. My eyes widened at the sight of it all. "What is this place? It's amazing."

"A couple of times a year they set this thing up. All the local shops and restaurant owners, artists, and whoever else is interested can set up shop right here in the middle of town for a few days. People come from all over to check it out. Pretty cool, right?"

Watching in awe as a man dressed in medieval clothing juggled daggers I agreed, "It's absolutely perfect."

And it was perfect, and I loved it. But it also reminded me of all I'd missed out on being locked away from the world on the pack estate, and of all the things I'd never get to do or see as Marcus's wife, the alpha's mate.

The dark thought was immediately quashed as Paul threw his arm around my shoulders and pulled me close. "Come on. Let's take a look around."

We chatted and joked as we checked out all the little makeshift stores. We stopped at a huge cart covered in every type of accessory imaginable and took turns trying on tons of silly hats, god-awful scarves, and trendy sunglasses to see who could come up with the most creative combination. A few sightseers stopped to informally judge, and after a couple of tossups he topped my hot-pink sunhat, plaid winter scarf, and mint-green satin gloves that came up to my elbows by modeling a pinstriped Fedora, a baby-pink feather boa and some aviator glasses for me and a dozen or so sightseers. Watching him strut around in ridiculous, mismatched accessories made me laugh so hard I cried.

He pulled his sunglasses down to the bridge of his nose and peeked out over the top. "Sorry, Michaels. Looks like you lost out to my superb fashion sense. Better luck next time."

"Maybe you should give up music and try fashion school. I think you may have missed your calling," I teased as we cleaned up the mess we'd made. After we thanked the cart owner for putting up with us, we headed out to our next destination.

Wandering side by side we brushed shoulders, and when he laced his fingers through mine my heart fluttered and I couldn't remember the last time I'd been so content. I reveled in the newfound feeling. Paul slowed down and pointed toward an ice cream vendor. "How about some of that? You can't come to a place like this and not eat ice cream. It's like a rule."

I smiled up at him and nodded my head. "It's my all-time favorite rule. Ice cream is a must."

We ordered two waffle cones filled with Rocky Road and found a bit of shade to sit under and relax while we enjoyed our treat. Sitting cross-legged, facing each other, we talked about trivial things like the weather, our favorite things to do in the summer, and the importance of choosing just the right ice cream flavor.

At one point he asked me if I had plans to go off to college, a perfectly normal question for someone who just graduated from high school. I froze. I had no idea how to answer him. I finally mumbled something about being undecided, and after he shot me an odd look, he quickly changed the subject.

Once that disastrous moment was over, he kept things light and playful, which both relieved and confused me.

When the crowd thinned out and most of the vendors began to pack up shop, we headed back to the record store where I'd left my car. I didn't want to leave, but I knew I couldn't stay. The real world was waiting for me back home, and I'd have to return to it sooner or later.

I leaned my back against the driver's side door and faced the guy who had managed to completely steal my heart in less than twenty-four hours. I had a feeling that when I drove away from here I'd be leaving a part of me behind, a part I might never get back.

A storm of butterflies took flight inside my stomach as he placed his hands on my hips and stared into my eyes. "I'd like to see you again, Lillian."

A nervous and unsure-sounding *okay* slipped out of my mouth, and his usually carefree eyes suddenly looked unsure too.

"Look, I'm not going to stand here and act like I have this amazing gift for reading people, but I have a feeling there's a lot more to you than you let on. And you're not up for sharing, I get it. I won't push you. You can tell me all about yourself when you're ready. I just want to make sure I *do* see you again."

The sincerity of his words touched me somewhere deep inside but stung me just the same. He knew I was holding back, that I had something to hide…and he somehow understood not to push me. My cheeks flushed at the thought that he actually wanted to see me again, and I searched the depths of my brain trying to figure out how I could make it happen.

I was just about to respond when he lowered his head to kiss me. He stopped for a second just before his lips met mine, as if giving me the chance to decide. There was no way in hell I was going to stop him, though, and to show him that I'd made my decision I wrapped my hands around the back of his neck. When he finally pressed his lips to mine, I melted into his embrace and threaded my fingers through the back of his hair.

The slow, sensual kiss sent my hormones into overdrive, and I'd never been more turned on in my life.

All too soon he pulled away and asked, "Will you call me?"

Needing a moment to regain my senses, I nodded my head in reply.

"And Friday, we have a gig at a local club. Wanna come watch us play?"

Again, I nodded my head.

"If I keep asking questions, will you keep saying yes? Because I can keep going."

I laughed, nodded my head, and said, "Probably."

"Then, do you promise you'll call? And before you answer, just know you can't say you will and then don't. Another rule."

His eyes lit up as I nodded my head once more and said, "You and your rules. Do you just make this shit up as you go?"

He shrugged his shoulders and replied, "I'm not at liberty to say. You know, it being a rule and all." Before I could respond, he brushed his soft lips against mine again and then whispered, "Don't forget to call. You promised."

Chapter 10

Thank God for Mrs. Walker and my mother's constant wedding questions and planning or I wouldn't have made it through the week. I'd been literally losing my mind waiting for Friday to finally arrive, and now that it was here, I was scared shitless.

For most of the week I'd immersed myself in the role of an excited bride-to-be and followed Marcus's mother around almost every day. And while I was pretty sure Mrs. Walker wouldn't be too happy if she knew that her floral selections and menu choices were helping to keep my mind off seeing Paul again tonight, I figured what she didn't know wouldn't hurt her. It's not like she'd been thinking about what would hurt me. When Marcus stopped by the florist earlier that day to meet his mother and me because he "just had to see the flowers we picked out," I thought for sure Mrs. Walker would notice how uncomfortable the two of us were making decisions about a day we were both dreading, but she didn't. If she did notice, she didn't care.

Marcus stuck around for all of ten minutes, reassured his mother that the centerpieces were lovely, and then promptly excused himself. Before he ran off, he claimed that he'd be busy with work for the rest of the day and wouldn't be around until late tonight, and he'd be so tired that he probably wouldn't be very good company.

Well, that's one hell of a relief, I thought, *since I was heading to Taos to see another guy.*

I knew that sneaking around behind Marcus's back was wrong, but I'd shoved that little notion so far back into the dark recesses of my mind that the guilt only bubbled up every once in a while. All I had to do was spend about three minutes alone with Marcus to remember that my life had practically been stolen from under me, and maybe this was my way of taking just a smidgen of it back.

Not that it was *that* easy. On my way back to Red Ridge last Sunday, I'd only made it about ten miles down the road before all the happy, fluttery feelings from Paul's kiss were swallowed whole by the nasty little bugger named guilt. Suddenly I was overcome with shame, being that I was now not only a liar but a cheater too, and I had no idea how to handle it. I had to pull over on the side of the road so my mini panic attack didn't make me have an accident.

Needless to say, I felt like total scum. But that all changed somewhere around Wednesday when I slapped on my happy face and said and did everything I was supposed to, and surprise, surprise, it wasn't enough.

My mother bitched me out for not being "excited" enough in front of Mrs. Walker, and then Marcus gave me the second lame excuse in a row about working late. Like I didn't know exactly what he was doing—or should I say *who* he was doing, since I'd bet it was Noel in spite of anything he said. It was after that miserable day and an even worse evening that I picked up the phone and pulled out the flyer that I had stuffed under my mattress. From then on, I was done feeling guilty. Never in a million years did I ever think that I'd be the type to cheat, but here I was and could honestly say that I didn't feel that bad about it.

The whole time I was getting ready, I racked my brain for a plausible excuse for leaving tonight and staying out so late. I had nothing! I was just hoping that my parents wouldn't ask when I made my getaway. On top of that, I had no idea what to wear and the act of searching through my closet was making me nuts, so I just put on a white tank, my black floral baby-doll dress, and my Docs. That would just have to do.

Before I left, I peeked downstairs and saw that my parents' bedroom door was closed, so I grabbed my purse and keys and walked out of the house like I always did when going to Marcus's. Free and clear...at least until I got home.

Honestly, I had no idea what they'd do if they caught me. Surely they wouldn't rat me out, if only because it could ruin their chance of marrying into the alpha's family. They wouldn't be protecting me. They'd be protecting themselves. But I wasn't foolish enough to believe that they'd just sweep it under the rug either. There was no doubt in my mind that there'd be serious consequences. I could only hope that I'd never have to find out what those were.

The drive from the estate into Taos was only about forty minutes, so I wasn't worried about driving there by myself. On the other hand, I was a little apprehensive about going into a club alone. I didn't have much of a choice, though. It wasn't like I could ask a friend from the pack to come with me while I cheated on their alpha, and thanks to Marcus I didn't have any domestic friends. Not any close ones, anyway. My only possible option was Tiffany, but I figured it would be safer just going alone.

Paul asked me to come a little early, which in his line of work meant 10:00 p.m., and I pulled in at 10:07. Perfect timing. But if my shaking hands gripping the steering wheel were any indicator, it would be safe to say that my nerves were definitely getting the best of me. As I pulled into a tight parking space of the 17th Street Bar, I knew that I needed to calm down before I made an ass out of myself.

I forced myself out of the car, straightened my dress, and walked up to the building trying to at least appear like I knew what I was doing. A pretty girl with pink hair, about my age, was working the door.

"You must be Lillian?" she said, surprising the hell out of me. I popped my knuckles and nodded my head in response. She motioned toward the door. "The band is setting up. Go on in."

Paul must have told her to look for me. My heart swelled at the thought. It had been so long since anyone actually considered my feelings, and it kind of made me feel important, which significantly improved my comfort level.

The bar was open and a decent number of patrons were there, but the lights had yet to be turned down low and the music was just background noise. As soon as I walked through the door and turned the first corner, I saw him. More delectable than ever, he stood on the stage looking like he'd just walked out of one of the many fantasies I'd dreamt up over the last week. He wore those same slim-fit black pants from the first time I'd seen him, and his blond hair was once again dyed red. I could have stood there all night just watching him from afar, but he looked up just in time to catch me admiring the view.

I swear time slowed to a crawl as he slipped his guitar over his head, revealing the tiniest peek of smooth tanned skin covering a firm, flat stomach. He hopped off the stage and jogged my way with that killer smile on his face that never failed to cause my pulse to race.

"You made it," he said, just before his lips met mine in a searing kiss that ended all too soon. It completely caught me off-guard but in the best possible way. It was crazy that we'd only kissed once before, yet Paul already felt comfortable enough to just walk up to me and do it in the middle of the empty dance floor. Maybe it was because he was the passionate-performer type, or maybe it was just his personality. He just seemed so incredibly sure of himself and at ease in his own skin. For that, I envied him.

"You look amazing," he whispered as he pulled me tighter against him. It was times like this when being a werewolf was a definite advantage; his scent washed over me, and every molecule in my body fired up and felt alive. I couldn't help but turn in to his hug and breathe in his deliciousness.

Paul let his arm fall and he grabbed my hand. "Come on. Let me introduce you to some of my friends."

He led me toward a large table set off to the side that was obviously reserved for the band. There were three girls and a guy sitting there already. I met Jennifer, the lead singer's girlfriend, then Stephanie, who was dating the other guitar player, and Jackie and Kirt, the drummer's brother and sister. They were all smiles and handshakes and made me feel like part of the group straightaway.

"I gotta go get set up. You going to be okay here?" Paul asked.

"Go, she'll be fine. We will tell her everything she needs to know about you," Kirt teased. Everyone laughed at the dirty look Paul shot him.

I gave Paul a little shove and told him that I would be fine. Before he left, though, he cupped my face in his hand and kissed me again. Purely on its own, my body sagged against him and my eyes closed. I didn't know how he did it, but somehow he made me forget everyone else in the room.

The band began its set just as the club started to fill up. I must admit that the Spastic Bambis were really good. Paul's friends were super-friendly, and not one of them had anything bad to say about Paul. He wasn't a jerk, he wasn't arrogant, he wasn't a womanizer, et cetera, et cetera. From what I could tell, he really was the perfect guy, which kind of made what I was doing here even worse. Would a guy like him have anything to do with me if he knew I was engaged to another? I knew the answer to that question, and it stung.

As I watched Paul play, my mind sorted through all the reasons why I should get up and leave, throw away Paul's number and forget that I'd ever met him. The first obvious problem was that I'm not human. Then there was the matter of a diamond ring that should be on my finger instead of in my jewelry box. The list could go on and on, but those two were so huge, they were enough all on their own.

I had almost convinced myself that I should sneak out the back when Paul's spine-tingling voice filled the air. This time he sang a cover of "Runaway Train," and I could barely breathe much less convince my legs to carry me away from him. His voice sounded so desperate and lost that I wanted to cry. It was like he was singing every single thing I was feeling.

I stared, unable to tear my eyes away from him. When his eyes weren't closed, they were on me, and something intense and real was passing between us. I was almost relieved when the song came to an end. I felt exposed, like Paul could see right through me, like all my secrets were on display, and I could no longer hide behind my lies.

I remained glued to my stool, and before I knew it was last call and the band was finished for the night. Only vaguely aware of the conversation taking place at the table, I watched as Paul carefully packed up his equipment. The girl with the pink hair handed him a beer as he walked past the bar and straight over to me. He pulled up a barstool next to mine and sat so close that we were touching. He rested his arms on the table and turned his head so that he could look right at me. I didn't say anything, and neither did he. The moment was too raw, too intimate.

Before I could talk myself out of it, I leaned over and kissed him. His skin was warm and slick with perspiration. His lips were soft and tasted faintly of Bud Light. It was just a kiss. A simple pressing of lips together, but it confirmed what I already knew. I was falling hard and fast for this guy.

Paul introduced me to his band-mates, and we sat and chatted until well after closing. The 17th Street Bar was a regular Friday night gig for them, so they knew everyone there.

When the cleaning crew arrived, everyone decided to call it a night. I said goodbye to the group while Paul gathered his gear, and then I went with him to put it in his car. With everything packed up, it was time for us to say goodbye.

He leaned against my car door, and it just felt right to walk into his arms. The moment I pulled back to look up at him, his lips were on mine, and this kiss was unlike any of the others. It was hot and hard and had me grasping at his shoulders just to stay on my feet. His lips were laced with a kind of passion I'd never encountered. As his tongue explored my mouth, tasting all of me, my body grew eager and the need to touch more of him was clawing at me. I threw my arms around his neck and deepened our kiss even more, causing a sudden ache to begin building inside me.

Paul let his lips leave mine, and I started to protest but fell silent as they moved down my neck and then back up to my ear. "Stay with me tonight?" he whispered, and the desire in his voice was unmistakable. He lifted my chin and looked into my eyes. *"Stay with me."*

I wanted to, oh God, I wanted to. There was nothing in the universe that I wanted more, but I couldn't. I couldn't give myself to him when technically I belonged to another. It wasn't right, and it wasn't fair to either of us. Plus, I couldn't bear to think about what my pack would do if they found out about Paul. I couldn't let that happen. I needed to leave, if for no other reason than to protect him.

I closed my eyes and rested my head on his chest. I could feel our heartbeats begin to slow down together.

"It's okay," he said softly.

I looked up at him. "I'm sorry. I can't, but there is nothing I would rather do."

We stood there in each other's arms for a few more minutes before I told him that I had to go. Paul opened my car door, and I got in and lowered my window. He leaned in and kissed me goodbye.

"Call me and let me know you made it home, okay?" he said.

I smiled and promised to call. After one more sweet small kiss I drove away.

Chapter 11

I fell back onto my bed with the phone glued to my ear and peeked over at the alarm clock on my nightstand. *Shit! Two-thirty a.m.?* I needed to get to bed, but listening to the sound of Paul's voice kept sleepiness far at bay.

"So, can you make it tomorrow? Can't wait to see you again."

"I'll be there," I assured him. And I would. Nothing was going to keep me away from the 17th Street Bar, because I couldn't wait to see him either. We'd spent almost every night this week talking on the phone until well into the early morning hours, and I'd even managed to sneak away to meet him for lunch on Wednesday. The intense feeling I felt for him grew stronger every minute of every day, and all I could think about was when I'd get to be with him again.

"I'll be waiting. I miss you. A lot."

My eyes closed as the sincerity of his words washed over me. "I miss you too. I better go, but I'll see you tomorrow. Ten o'clock?"

"Yeah, ten o'clock… Until then, goodnight, Lillian Michaels. Sweet dreams."

The tone of his voice left no doubt in my mind that they would be very sweet indeed.

*****

Unlike last Friday, I wasn't able to slip out of my house so easily. I headed downstairs and ran right into my father just before I made my escape, but he was a far better option than my mother.

"You headed to Marcus's?"

Picking up my purse and keys, I said the only thing that came to mind. "Yeah, he rented a few movies so I'll probably be home late."

The relief that flashed across Dad's face cut deep, and I had to turn away before the deception in my eyes gave me away. Before I shut the door I heard, "I'm glad to see you two spending time together. Have fun."

I couldn't find it in myself to respond, so I left without a word and said a silent prayer that my parents wouldn't call the Walkers looking for me.

Alone in the car on the open road, my guilty conscience that occasionally rears its ugly head made an unwelcome appearance. After a minor freak-out over the prospect of being busted by my parents before the night's end, my thoughts turned to Paul and all the truths I couldn't tell him. Somewhere along the way my cheating on Marcus with Paul had flip-flopped and it felt more like I was cheating on Paul instead. Even though Marcus had barely laid a finger on me since the announcement of our engagement, the fact of the matter was that I was still engaged and Paul had no idea.

By the time I arrived in Taos, I'd convinced myself that I was the most horribly wretched person on planet Earth. I was a lying, cheating fraud who didn't deserve a guy like Paul. Maybe I did deserve to be stuck in a loveless marriage with Marcus Walker.

Before I literally hyperventilated, I took a sharp turn into a Taco Bell parking lot. I knew what I needed to do. I needed to turn my car around, step on the gas, and try to forget what it felt like to be in Paul's arms. But I couldn't. I'd promised Paul that I'd come, and I couldn't break that promise. It was like a rule.

As I pulled back out onto the street, I made a vow to myself. Tonight, no matter how much it hurt, I'd end things with Paul. I couldn't be with him. I'd always known my time with him was only temporary, but along with a lot of other things I'd rather ignore I'd chosen not to think about it. All I had left was tonight, so I buried my grief deep down inside before I entered the bar for the last time.

When I rounded the corner, I saw all the same faces from last Friday sitting around the table, but Paul was nowhere in sight. On my way over, a long lean arm came from behind and wrapped around my waist. Suddenly my feet were off the ground, and Paul was spinning me around as he kissed the back of my neck. He breathed into my hair and said, "God, I missed you like crazy."

Once my feet were firmly back on the ground, I turned and threw my arms around his neck. "Not as much as I missed you."

Our bodies melded together as our lips connected. I sank into him and struggled to stay on two feet, but his arm snaked around my lower back to hold me up and he kissed the living daylights out of me right there in the middle of the bar. Before his lips left mine, he lifted me off the ground once more and tugged playfully on my bottom lip with his teeth. Still holding my body firmly against his he whispered, "You wanna get out of here? I'm sure no one will miss me."

I was just about to answer when the hooting and hollering began. We both turned our attention to the table near the stage and laughed as his group of friends cheered us on. I muttered, "They will definitely notice."

Paul put me down. "Guess it's too late to slip out the back then?"

I grabbed his hand and led him over to the table. "Come on, you have a show to do. But I'll be right here when it's over."

Everyone greeted me warmly as Paul pulled out a bar stool for me, and without even having to ask a waitress placed a Coke in front of me. Paul thanked her and then turned to his friends and said, "You all take care of my girl while I'm gone." After a quick peck on the cheek, he made his way to the stage.

There I sat, utterly entranced by a guy I'd only known for a short time. Somehow it already felt like a lifetime. His fingers moved deftly over the strings of his bass guitar, and it was like he was playing just for me. The anticipation of hearing his voice again was practically killing me, and when he finally took center stage, I almost jumped off my stool.

As he sang the first lines of Smashing Pumpkins' "Luna," I had to laugh at the irony of him singing about moonsongs. I swayed to the music and hummed along until his eyes cut to me as he sang, "'I'm in love with you, I'm in love with you, I'm in love with you.'"

Frozen in time, I gazed into his pale-blue eyes and lost myself in the words of a song about the moon and being in love. "'I'm in love with you. So in love. I'm in love with you,'" rang through the bar, and everything fell away except Paul and me. Completely connected, his eyes never left mine until the song ended and the crowd erupted.

I sat there in a hazy stupor for the remainder of his set. My mind couldn't string together a coherent thought, much less carry on an intelligent conversation with those around me. The band headed over to the table, and Paul wrapped his arm around me and kissed my cheek. After spending a few minutes with his friends, he whispered in my ear, "Wanna go outside?"

I nodded my head, and we politely excused ourselves.

Nervous energy coursed through every molecule of my being as I followed him out to his car. After his performance, I wasn't sure what to expect. Surely, those were just the words to a song he just happened to be singing. He wasn't professing his love for me. It didn't mean anything, right? He couldn't possibly love me. *Like* me? Sure. Love? No way.

Out of nowhere, a teeny-tiny voice in the back of my mind reminded me that I was supposed to be ending this, but as I watched him hop up on the hood of his Camaro, I tucked the pesky little thought away, at least for the time being.

He patted the spot next to him and admitted, "Sorry, but I kinda wanted you all to myself tonight."

Despite the fact that I was still in freak-out mode on the inside, a smile broke out across my face. I took a seat next to him and as calmly as possible said, "You won't hear me complaining."

He took my hand, and we chatted about nothing for a few minutes before he asked, "So, are you ever going to give me your number?"

With my nerves firing on all cylinders, I tried to come up with a reasonable excuse, but as usual I came up blank.

Paul squeezed my hand and explained, "It's okay. Really. I just want to be able to get in touch with you. I'm always waiting by my phone for my ever-mysterious girl to call."

Focused on the gravel below, I gave him the only answer I could. "I know, and I'm sorry. I just can't right now, okay?"

He let go of my hand and wrapped me in his arms. I laid my cheek against his chest and his chin rested on the top of my head. We breathed in unison as silence filled the air. I feared my answer wasn't enough, and just as he began to speak, I braced myself for heartbreak.

"I said I wouldn't push you, and I'm trying really hard to stick to my word. It's just, I really like you a lot. To be honest, I think I more than like you, and for some reason I have a bad feeling that one day you may not call, and it kills me to think that you could just slip through my fingers like that."

He more than likes me. My heart soared at the thought, and I sat up to look into his eyes as I admitted, "I more than like you, too."

He lifted me up and pulled me into his lap. I thought he was going to kiss me, but he didn't. He just stared at me for the longest time before he spoke again. "I have to tell you something that I've wanted to tell you all week. But before I do, you have to know that

I'm crazy about you. Like, can't-get-you-off-of-my-mind-ever crazy about you, and I want to see you more, preferably every day. And you may think I'm completely nuts since we've only known each other for like two weeks, but I can't help it. And I don't want to help it because it just feels right."

He stopped and took in a deep breath before he kept going. "Okay, so I am supposed to be moving to Austin in a few days. Our band landed a killer gig at a bar on 6th Street. It will be every Thursday night starting at the end of July, and that city is full of other venues for us to play so it's a huge opportunity. Most of my stuff is packed, but…"

Even though I had planned that tonight would be my last night with Paul, tiny little pieces of my heart began to break off one by one as I listened to the words flooding out of his mouth, and I ended up cutting him off mid-sentence.

"So, you're leaving?" I asked, more to myself than to him as I imagined myself picking up all the tiny bits. Sure, I could collect them all, and over time somehow figure out how to fix my shattered heart, but would the tiny little shards ever fit back together the way they did before?

He shook his head no, and it took me a second to remember the question he was answering. "No, I'm not leaving. Not yet. Not before I know what this is." He moved his index finger back and forth between the two of us. "That's what I wanted to tell you. I want to spend every second I can with you, even if it's on your terms."

He wasn't leaving. He was staying. For me.

Suddenly, sitting sideways on his lap wasn't close enough. I lifted my body just a bit, moved one leg across his body and straddled him right there on the hood of his car. Yes, I'd promised myself I would end this tonight, but I couldn't bring myself to do it. Instead, I decided then and there to add another lie to the list. This time at least it was to myself.

Without an ounce of uncertainty, my eager lips crushed his and then parted to allow his tongue access. Instantly, our kisses were needy and demanding, and my last little bit of rational thought blew away in the summer breeze. I traced my fingers up his arms and down his back. Once they reached the bottom of his shirt, I slipped them inside and ran my fingertips up his finely-toned stomach and chest. When he shuddered under my touch, I deepened our kiss even more, needing to somehow be even closer.

His fingers untangled from my hair and slid down my neck. It was my turn to shudder as his fingers lightly touched my breasts on their way to my waist. Those sexy hands pulled me toward him, and he trailed kisses down my neck as he ran them up the sides of my body, stopping just underneath my bra. His lips found mine again, and my heaving chest pressed against him as our embrace became more urgent as each second passed.

If he'd asked me in that moment to go back to his apartment I wouldn't have denied him. I wanted him badly, and a sad little moan escaped my lips when he pulled away.

"It pains me to say this, but we should stop before I haul your ass into the backseat of my car."

I pouted, and he laughed. Tugging gently on my bottom lip with his teeth he smiled. "It's almost closing. You want to head inside for a few?"

I couldn't hide the sadness in my voice as I answered, "I should probably just head home."

With the tip of his finger, he lifted my chin to find my downcast eyes. "But you'll call, right?"

I couldn't stand the thought of never seeing him again. I was supposed to be breaking things off. This was supposed to be it, the last time. This couldn't be it, though, not yet. One day I'd have to let him go, but it wasn't going to be tonight. "Yeah, I'll call."

He kissed me softly before I got in my car. He stood there and watched as I backed up and pulled out of the parking spot. I glanced in my rearview mirror, hesitated for a moment, and then drove away.

*****

All the lights in my house were off when I got home. As quietly as possible I shut my car door and tiptoed up to the porch. I opened the front door, left the lights off, and snuck inside. Using the lightest of footsteps, I made my way up the stairs…and froze as soon as my bedroom door came into view.

Chapter 12

When I saw the light peeking out from under my bedroom door, I knew I was busted. I could only hope it was my mom and not Marcus in there waiting. Whoever it was would be able to smell Paul all over me, and I'd have no choice but to tell them the truth.

I opened my door and was only slightly relieved to see my mom sitting on my bed. She was holding my necklace with Marcus's alpha ring on it in one hand, my engagement ring in the other. She definitely smelled Paul on me.

"Mom, let m—"

She raised her hand, signaling me to stop talking before she interrupted. "Don't, Lily. Just don't." Her tone was harsh, and her eyes narrowed, marked with a mixture of anger and disappointment. Well aware of the ass-chewing I was about to get, I walked in and fell into my chair near the window.

She stood up and moved to stand in front of me. "I don't understand you, Lily. Marcus is a good guy. He is our alpha for crying out loud. He chose you, and you have the nerve to be out gallivanting all over town like a floozy?"

"Mom, that's not fair—"

"Don't talk to me about fair. This family has worked very hard to make sure that you are happy—"

It was my turn to cut her off. I shot up from my chair, forcing my mother to take a step back, and threw my purse on my bed. "Yeah, I know all about how hard you worked, Mom. Your little arrangement for me. You couldn't have a boy, so you basically sold me to the highest bidder—"

I didn't even see her hand before it came down hard across my face. My hand flew to my cheek and tears stung at my eyes. I backed up and sat back in my chair with my head in my hands. My mother sat back on my bed.

"It wasn't like that," she said, sounding dejected, as if she were the one who'd just gotten slapped across the face.

"I don't love him, Mom. He doesn't love me."

"Don't be silly. You're just nervous. Marcus adores you," she countered.

"Marcus adored me when he was seventeen. Now we barely speak. He's the one who told me about the arrangement. He doesn't want to marry me, Mom. He's only going through with it because he thinks he has to."

She *had* to know that was true. It couldn't be a surprise. Anyone who was around us long enough could see that we were no longer the young couple in love, who couldn't get enough of each other. But it didn't seem to matter.

"Lily," she said, taking a shaky breath, "you are marrying Marcus in less than two months. You will smile as you walk down that aisle…"

I rolled my eyes at her complete lack of sympathy. Could she really be so cold that she would sacrifice the happiness of her only child to protect her position in the pack?

"Do not roll your eyes at me, young lady! I am dead serious about this. We made this arrangement for you to protect you and your future. Without an enforcer in our family, where would that leave us? We were not born to be followers, Lily. We are leaders. You are a leader. You will be the alpha female of this pack very soon. It's time you start acting like it."

After a few deep calming breaths, she stood and walked over to me and lightly touched the cheek that she'd slapped. "My baby. You need to trust me. You and Marcus will be fine. All couples go through tough times. It will pass."

I did everything I could to keep the tears from falling. "What if it doesn't? What if we really don't love each other? What if we can't?" I asked, wanting an honest answer.

"Not all marriages are built on love, sweetie. Life isn't a fairy tale. We don't all get swept off our feet by some guy riding on a white horse. And sometimes love just takes time," she answered.

Mothers weren't supposed to tell you these things. I wasn't naive. I knew that marriage wasn't a guaranteed happy-ever-after, but shouldn't it feel that way in the beginning at least? If we weren't happy now, was there any hope for us at all?

My mom gave me her hand and pulled me to my feet. "One thing that will definitely ruin this marriage before it even starts is infidelity. It needs to stop. If Marcus and his family, heaven forbid, were to find out about this, what do you think would happen? Marcus would never allow that man to live. Your own father would probably have to be the one to take care of it. You would be ruined. We would be ruined. Think about someone beside yourself for once. Lily, if you actually believe that you care about this guy, it needs to stop now, before anyone else knows of your betrayal."

I just sat there, stunned and silent, as her words sank in.

"Okay, darling?" Mom asked.

I didn't have anything left in me, so I just nodded my head. Mom smoothed my hair with her hand and said, "Good. Go take a long, hot shower to get that domestic's stench off you, put your engagement ring back on your finger, and get a good night's sleep. Everything will seem better in the morning."

As soon as I stepped into the shower, the tears began to fall. As much as I hated to admit it, she was right. This was all my fault. I did this. Because I was stupid and selfish, I'd put Paul's life at risk. What was I thinking? I should have never called him, and I definitely shouldn't have gone to see him. Now the memories of his smiles, the way he looked at me when he sang, and the way his arms felt as he held me close would forever be in my heart. Those memories would haunt me always. What it felt like to kiss him, to be consumed by passion from just the touch of his lips would serve as a constant reminder of what I didn't have, what I never would.

I knew I'd never feel that way about Marcus. Knowing that crushed me. I didn't want a marriage of power and agreement. Of obligation. I wanted one filled with passionate kisses and Rocky Road ice cream and songs about love.

I went to bed knowing what I should do. Paul deserved more than my secrecy and lies, and I hated myself for dragging him into my fucked-up world. I'd just got so caught up in it all that I never thought about the future we could never have. The harsh truth was that Paul and I could never really be together. Tomorrow, as much as it would kill me, I would end things. For real this time. This wishy-washy girl needed to get a damn grip on reality.

The sooner he was out of the picture, the easier it would be for me to focus on the future I was destined to have, the future I'd have to face whether I wanted to or not.

Chapter 13

My night was plagued with fretful dreams, and I tossed and turned until sunlight seeped through the crack between my curtains. I lifted my head to look at my clock and wondered if I'd ever really fallen asleep. My mother was dead wrong. Nothing looked better. Not one damn thing.

I lay around all morning watching mindless television and waited for the afternoon to roll around. My bedroom door was locked, and I didn't plan on leaving until I had to. Both my parents—first my mom and an hour later, my dad—came up and knocked on my door. When I didn't acknowledge them, they stood there talking through my door asking if I was okay, if I was hungry, and begging me to come out. *No.*

Huddled under my covers in the confines of my bed, I stared at my tiny television. A repeat of *Yo MTV Raps* filled the screen, but it might as well have been snow because I couldn't focus on anything; not when my world was crumbling around me.

Finally, my clock read 12:00 p.m., so I reached over and dialed the number that would forever be burned into my memory. Paul answered on the third ring, sounding a bit out of breath. He was on his way out the door, he said, but he agreed to meet me at his apartment later so I took down the directions and settled in for another long wait.

*****

Hours later, my father knocked on my door once again. I ignored him.

"Lillian, you're going to have to come out of there at some point. And you need to eat, honey." Pause. Knock. "Lillian, do you hear me?"

I threw my flip-flop at the door in response.

"Okay…well, your mother and I are heading over to the Walkers' to meet with the Stantons about Phillip and his move to enforcer. You're welcome to join us." Pause. "Okay…just please eat something while we're gone. Your mother and I are worried about you."

I put my television on mute and listened intently for the front door to close behind them. Once I was alone, I threw back my covers and headed to the shower.

*****

Completely numb, I drove straight to Paul's apartment in Taos. I was so out of it that I could hardly remember how I'd gotten there. Just like I learned to do with my guilty conscience, I'd bottled up all of my feelings and tucked them away somewhere deep inside of myself. It was like my brain knew that I couldn't physically handle the chaotic mess brewing inside of me.

Before I got out of the car, I checked my makeup in the visor mirror. All the concealer and mascara in the world couldn't mask the misery in my eyes. There was nothing I could do about it, so I shut the visor, dragged myself out of the car, and headed to apartment 1173.

The door swung open, and Paul's huge grin instantly vanished as he took in the disheveled mess on his doorstep. He pulled me inside, wrapped his arms around me and said, "Hey, are you okay? Tell me what's wrong."

There, in his arms, the bottle containing every emotion within me shattered and I broke down in tears. I'd never felt anything like this before. Never had I been this upset, this broken, and I had no idea how to handle it. Flooded by my pent-up emotions, I completely lost it, and my shaky legs gave out from beneath me.

Paul's strong arms stopped me from collapsing to the floor as he slowly lowered both of our bodies to the ground. Never loosening his grasp, he pulled me up against him. I sat sideways between his legs with my head against his chest. He ran his fingers through my hair as I continued to sob.

"Lillian, please talk to me. You can tell me. There's nothing you could say that would change the way I feel about you."

I closed my eyes, wishing his words could be true. He just sat there holding me, patiently waiting for my tears to slow. I could hardly breathe through my choking sobs. He gently rubbed my back and assured me, "It's okay. Whatever it is, it's going to be okay."

When my breathing finally slowed, Paul lifted my head, so he could look into my eyes. "Please, Lillian. Let me help you. I promise that whatever it is you can tell me. It's killing me to see you this way."

He waited for me to respond, willing me with his eyes to say something, but I couldn't. The words were all jumbled up in my head. When my eyes drifted back to the floor, he took my face in his hands and begged, "Please look at me. I have no idea what this is about, but you need to know something before you say what I think you're going to say. I've fallen in love with you. Do you hear me? I love you, Lillian Michaels, more than I've ever loved anyone. I love all of you, everything about you. Even the part that you keep locked away. I think I fell in love with you the moment I saw you in the crowd at the music festival. And I know we haven't known each other long, but I can't lose you. Not when I can't imagine my life without you."

Silent tears continued down my face as I let his heartfelt confession sink in. He loved me, all of me. But that couldn't really be true because there was a huge part of me that he could never know. The hardest part of all was that I loved him too. I just couldn't admit it, not even to myself. Not until now.

I opened my mouth to tell him, but I couldn't say it out loud. To my surprise, other words came out instead. "You wouldn't love me if you really knew me…if you knew the truth."

Hurt flashed across his face, but then his body stiffened and his eyes narrowed on me as he argued, "You don't know that. How will you ever know that if you don't give me a chance? You can leave here tonight, holding on to your secret, and run away from your feelings for me, or you can trust me, tell me what's going on and give me the chance to show you how much I love you. I just want to be with you. Give me a chance to show you that nothing else matters."

I pushed myself up from off the floor. I needed some space. His nearness confused me. I turned my back to him and prepared myself to explain that I couldn't tell him everything, that there were things about me he could never know.

I took a few steps away and breathed deeply just before the words I meant to keep hidden exploded from my mouth. "I'm engaged. But I don't love him. In fact, I kind of hate him. He's an arrogant son of a bitch who hates me too. It's an arranged marriage, which I know sounds completely ridiculous in this day and age, but that's exactly what it is. Arranged. Our parents are forcing us to get married. Guess it's kind of obvious that I don't live in a typical American family. Far from it actually. I'm so sorry, Paul. I should have never dragged you into any of this, but I screwed up. I fell so hard for you, and I was selfish…*am* selfish. I didn't want to let you go. Please believe me when I say I don't want to marry him. I want to be with you…but I can't."

Paul stared up at me, eyes wide. For several seconds we just watched each other in silence. Then, he stood and walked toward me. Standing directly in front of me, he asked, "Engaged?"

I slightly nodded my head but didn't speak.

"Why can't you just leave? You're an eighteen-year-old adult living in America. They can't *force* you to do anything that you don't want to do. That really is a rule."

My eyes filled up with tears. He would never understand. Yes, they could, and they would. But how could I explain something like that to him, a human, who knew nothing about werewolves and pack laws?

He reached out and took my hands in his. "I'm serious, Lillian. You don't have to do this."

"Yes, I do. Because there is more. One more thing I haven't told you."

His eyes met mine, and the confusion and sadness in them caused my chest to tighten.

"Paul…I'm a werewolf."

Chapter 14

Oh my God! What did I just do?

Paul's beautiful face gradually drained of color as I spilled my secrets without stopping to think of the consequences. "Say something, Paul. Anything. Tell me to leave. Tell me you hate me. Just say something, please," I begged with tears in my eyes as he stood silently in front of me. He couldn't even look at me.

Still avoiding eye contact, he ran a hand through his hair. "Jesus, Lillian. If you don't want to tell me the truth then don't, but are you really going to stand here and make up some crazy shit just to push me away?" His voice was laced with anger, and I shouldn't have been surprised that he didn't believe me, but I was.

"I'm not making this up, Paul. I am a werewolf. Trust me, I wish I was making up crazy shit, but it's true. And I'm not insane if that's what you're thinking."

The condescending laugh that escaped his lips felt like a shot to the gut.

"Oh, good to know. My 'werewolf' girlfriend isn't insane. Thanks, I feel better already."

When I didn't reply, the realization that I was dead serious must have struck. Once again, his face turned a ghostly white, and he stumbled backward. My heart broke a little more with each step he took. He reached out his hand and grabbed the wall for support. I wanted to run away. Seeing Paul suffer from something I said was more than I could stand, but I also couldn't leave until he heard me out. He needed to know everything. Most importantly, he needed to know that my confession had left him in danger.

"Please, Paul, listen to me…"

I stopped as he raised one hand and held the other to his stomach. Without a word, he turned and walked out of the room.

When I heard the bathroom door shut and lock, I walked through his bedroom and stood outside of where he'd disappeared. I heard him talking to himself, but I couldn't make out the words.

The water turned on and off, but he didn't come out. I knocked lightly. When he didn't respond, I turned around and went to sit down on his bed, but once there I couldn't sit. I just stood there, staring down at his dark-brown comforter and crumpled beige sheets and knowing what I needed to do. Well, sort of.

If Paul wouldn't hear me out, I'd just have to make him listen. I would not let anything happen to him because of my stupidity and impulsiveness. Even if he never wanted to see me again, I had to make sure he understood that he could never repeat what I'd said. Even if he didn't believe me, he could never tell anyone that his crazy ex thought she was a werewolf. It would cost him his life if the wrong person heard. But how was I going to make sure he understood everything he needed to understand?

I was running my hand down his bedspread when Paul emerged from the bathroom with a wild expression on his face. "Show me," he said.

"Paul, you need to hear me out. You could be in troub—"

"Show me, Lillian!" he practically shouted. It was a tone he'd never used with me before.

"I'll just scare you even more, Paul. Please," I begged. I didn't want him to think of me that way. I wanted to be the Lillian he'd fallen in love with, even if we couldn't be together. Was that so wrong?

Paul took two hesitant steps toward me then stopped. He lowered his steely eyes and stared straight through me. "Please, Lillian. I need to know that what you're saying is real or if you're out of your mind. I need to *know,"* he demanded.

This was not a good idea. I suddenly wished I could just let him continue to think I was crazy, but I had to protect him. I had to do this. I dragged my hands through my hair and turned away from him. I took a few steps and then forcefully popped my knuckles. Turning back to him I said, "Okay. Okay, Paul, but please don't freak out. Okay? I will not hurt you," I added before I hurried over and took his hands in mine. "Do you hear me? I will not hurt you. Tell me you understand."

Paul nodded and removed his hands from mine, leaving me feeling cold and rejected.

When I told him that I needed to remove my clothes, he shot me a skeptical look but then turned and faced the bathroom door. Reluctantly I stripped and shifted into wolf form.

In the middle of his bedroom, unable to speak, I made a small noise that came out as a pitiful whimper, as I needed to get his attention. Paul slowly turned. His eyes widened, and his jaw dropped. I could tell that he was trying very hard to stay calm, but I could smell the fear rolling off him. I sat back, hoping that he would fear me less that way.

"You were telling me the truth? You're a fucking *wolf?*" he said more to himself than to me. His head fell back as he spoke to the ceiling, "Please, God, tell me this isn't happening. Tell me I'm the one who's crazy. There can't be a freakin' wolf in my bedroom." Then he just stood silent for the longest time staring at me like he was terrified of me but at the same time afraid to look away.

After a while Paul seemed to gather himself. He inched his way closer, but it was still too much. I could hear his pulse begin to race out of control, and he stopped.

I couldn't take it anymore. In this form, all my senses were heightened and overly sensitive. His panicked breathing and pounding heart, the smell of his fear, the redness around his eyes were tearing me up inside. I felt myself begin to twist—

Shit! Oh shit! Something was wrong. I was fighting to maintain my form for the first time since I was sixteen. Growing more and more desperate, I got up and tried to hide from him on the other side of his bed. My body contorted and seized, and I recognized that my change was happening without my desire. I had no control.

Suddenly, I was lying on Paul's floor, naked. I turned on my side and hugged my knees to my chest as my breaths became choking sobs. My world was imploding, and there was nothing I could do to stop it. Nothing at all.

I jumped when I felt Paul wrap his comforter around me. I tugged the blanket tightly around my shoulders and pushed myself up to sit on my knees. Through my tears, I saw Paul kneeling too. He waited before me with a mixture of curiosity and disgust in his eyes.

"You...you can't tell anyone," I cried. "They, my pack, will kill you if they find out that I told you." Paul tried to shush me, but I had to get this out. "I promise, I'll leave and never come back, but please understand: If you tell anyone, they will kill you. I don't care what they do to me, but please don't let them hurt you. I know that I've ruined everything. You could never love me now, but you have to know how sorry I am. I'm so, so sorry," I cried.

He inched closer and gently yet somewhat hesitantly ran his hand up and down my back. "Shush. Shush...calm down," he soothed. All too soon he stopped, though, and ran his hand through his hair. "I don't know how I'm supposed to react or what to say. There are a million questions running through my head right now."

"You can ask me anything. I don't have anything left to hide."

He stood up and began pacing his room. After popping his neck and every knuckle in his hands, he shook them out and stopped in front of me. I looked up at him as he let out a huge huff.

"Okay, were you born this way or bitten? How many werewolves are there in New Mexico? Are they everywhere? If werewolves exist, what else? Are vampires real too?" he asked, not pausing between questions for me to actually answer. Then he started mumbling to himself as he once again started nervously walking back and forth.

I watched knowing that this was it, that this was the last time I would ever see him. There was no way he would ever be able to accept this, much less forgive me for hurting him. I hugged his blanket tighter around me as the string of questions began again to fly out of his mouth. "What's the deal with full moons? Do you live longer than humans? Wait…are you immortal, or can you be killed? What about the whole silver bullet thing? Tell me that's just bullshit, right?"

I froze as the questions stopped and Paul stood over me waiting for me to say something. I tried but couldn't even remember the last question he'd asked. My entire body began to shake as my eyes once again filled with tears. I couldn't do this. I buried my face in the blanket and waited for him to tell me to leave.

Paul sat back down and pulled me to him. I laid my head on his chest, and he wiped my hair out of my face with his hand. "Look at me," he whispered. "Baby, look at me."

When I lifted my eyes, he smiled through his own tears. I reached over and wiped a tear from his cheek. He leaned into my touch.

"I promise to answer all of your questions if you give me the chance. I'm so sorry about everything. I messed everything up. I just—"

"Stop," he cut in. "I don't care what you are. I don't care that you're a…a werewolf, which, don't get me wrong, is absolutely mind-blowing, completely insane, but I don't care. I love you."

"But Paul—"

My words were silenced by the sweetest of kisses.

"Paul, I'm not—"

His lips returned to cut off my words again. He trailed little kisses up to my forehead and down my cheeks until he re-found my lips. This time, his kiss was heated and carried with it the salty taste of our tears.

I wrapped my arms around his neck and pulled him closer. I was overwhelmed by the velvety softness of his mouth as he took his time exploring mine. His hands traveled slowly down my back, taking the comforter down with them. I shivered as the cool air touched my overheated skin, and that familiar ache that only Paul could generate was back tenfold. I wanted him. I needed to have him closer, and when his hand skimmed down the side of my breast, my body felt absolutely explosive.

Paul's hands worked their way back up to my face, and he pulled me close for another firm, demanding kiss. He looked at me, asking with his eyes. I smiled and leaned over to whisper in his ear, "A million times, yes."

He lifted me off his lap and gently placed me beside him before he stood and reached to help me up. When I stood, the blanket dropped to the floor, and I smiled as Paul's eyes widened at the sight of me standing completely naked before him. He closed the distance between us, and before I knew it he lifted me into his arms and laid me back on his bed.

Chapter 15

My cheek rested against Paul's bare chest. I stared at the clock on his bedside table as I listened to his pulse return to normal. I had no idea what lay ahead, but I knew I had to get home soon before my mother rounded up a search party to locate her "missing" daughter.

I needed to go, but couldn't convince my limbs to move.

Paul kissed the top of my head and let out a sigh. "So, what now? What happens next?"

That was one of the many questions that I had absolutely no answer for. How could I ever go back to my life at the estate now? My voice shook as I answered honestly, "I don't know."

We lay there in silence for a long time. As I watched the numbers change on the clock, I listened to his heartbeat. The stillness of the room was unsettling, but I didn't have any answers to give him.

"Move to Austin with me. We can start over there, together. Just you and me. We can pack up and leave everything behind."

I lifted my heavy head and looked into his eyes. They were so full of hope that it caused my insides to stir. "You're crazy, you know that? You can't be serious."

He raised his eyebrows and said, "I've never been more serious about anything in my entire life. I mean it, Lillian. Let's just go. I've been saving every penny I've earned for months. We can get an apartment together and start a new life. You don't ever have to go back."

Holding the sheet against my body, I sat up. Keeping my back to him I answered, "Just leave? I can't just take off." Did he realize what he was asking me? Give up everything and everyone I ever knew?

He ran his fingers down my back before he spoke again. "Would you rather stay here and marry a man you don't love? Because that's what will happen if you stay. Life is too short to not take a few chances. Take a chance on us, and I'll do everything in my power to make sure you won't regret it."

I felt him sit up, but I continued to stare at the wall in front of me. Paul placed his hand on my shoulder and gently pulled backward, guiding my body so that I would turn and face him. The hopefulness in his eyes had faded, so I found it hard to look at him.

Thoughts whirled in my brain. New thoughts. He wasn't just saying this. He *wanted* me to go with him. I could tell. And just the thought that I could really be with Paul was so incredible…but I truly would be giving up everything I've ever known. I didn't understand how I could feel so excited about the idea of something and so terrified at the same time.

Paul tucked my hair behind my ear and asked, "Do you love me, Lillian? I mean, *really* love me?"

There was only one answer to that question, an answer I was more than certain of now. "Yes, I love you. I love you so much it scares me."

He cupped my face in his hands. "It scares the hell out of me too, but I love you more than words can say. And yes, it's crazy. I don't know how I can feel this way so soon, but I do. Crazy or not, I love you. Let's be crazy together. Let's leave this place behind. Come to Austin and be with me."

Suddenly it all became very clear. There was only one choice to make. It wasn't between Paul or Marcus. I was choosing me. I was choosing my one and only shot at ever being truly happy. Paul was everything for me. He was the one. So, crazy or not, I nodded my head.

"Okay, let's do it. Me and you."

He gathered me in his arms and pulled me on top of him. As his lips covered mine, I knew deep down that I'd made the best decision I could make. Right or wrong, no matter the consequences, I no longer belonged to the Red Ridge pack, or my parents, or Marcus Walker. I'd finally found where I truly belonged, and it was in the arms of Paul Wright.

Chapter 16

I could hardly fathom how much my life changed since the summer began. I had never even traveled outside of New Mexico, and in three short days I planned on hopping in a car and moving to Austin with Paul. That was the best part. I'd be with Paul, the man I loved, not here with Marcus, the guy I'd grown to despise. A strange but happy kind of nervousness filled my soul every time I thought about leaving the only home I'd ever known. Somehow I was simultaneously scared to death and completely exhilarated about leaving it all behind and starting over somewhere new, without my family, without my pack, without any kind of safety net at all. But I knew in my heart that Paul and I would make it because we had each other.

The only thing I had to do was avoid my parents and Marcus for the next seventy-two hours…which proved to be impossible because I was asked to join the Walkers for dinner at their house the very next evening. I thought about politely refusing, claiming that I had some pressing matter to attend, but of course Mother jumped in and accepted the invitation for me.

While I was in my room getting ready for the "big dinner," Mom came in without knocking.

"Is that what you're wearing?" she asked as she eyeballed the outfit I'd lain out on my bed. When I nodded she said, "Good. That skirt always looks nice on you."

I was sitting at my vanity finishing my makeup, and she walked up behind me. She placed her hands on my shoulders and looked at me through the mirror. "Did you take care of that little issue we discussed the other night? I'm assuming that's where you ran off to."

I set my mascara down and wiggled out from under her touch. "Yes. I did," I lied. Needing to put some distance between us, I stood and walked to the other side of the bed.

Mom smiled. "That's my girl. Now you need to make sure that Marcus knows that you are *completely committed* to him. You are completely committed to this marriage now, aren't you?"

Tomorrow night could not come soon enough. It was difficult to admit, even if it was just to myself, but I really didn't think that I was going to miss her.

"Yes, Mother," I stated flatly, showing no emotion whatsoever. I really didn't need to irritate her right now, but I couldn't help myself.

She got that cold, harsh look on her face that she reserved for times when she was really pissed. I readied myself for her wrath, but she completely threw me for a loop by leaning over, picking up a tube off the vanity and tossing it to me. With a glare that spoke volumes she spat, "You need more lip gloss, dear." Then she walked out of the room.

Dinner at the Walkers' wasn't as bad as I thought it would be, just a lot of pointless wedding talk. If everything went as planned, by August Paul and I would be happily settled in Texas and my time here would be a distant memory.

Mrs. Walker gushed when I agreed to wear her wedding gown. Why not? No need to say no when it was never going to happen anyway.

In no time, the evening came to an end and Marcus asked if I wanted him to walk me home.

"No, it's fine. I'm sure you're busy with pack business," I told him, sounding surprisingly accommodating, which must have caught him off guard. Was that disappointment in his eyes? I guessed he was the one who needed to get used to disappointment now!

"Are you sure?" he asked, clearly taken aback.

I walked over and gave him a friendly little hug. He leaned in to give me our typical goodbye kiss, but I turned my head and offered my cheek instead. My lips belonged to someone else, and I didn't care if I was still technically Marcus's fiancée, I wouldn't cheat on Paul. Leaving Marcus befuddled, I walked out of his house all alone.

Mom had already retired to her room by the time I got home, but Dad was still up watching *SportsCenter*. Seeing him, the big bad pack enforcer looking so serene in his easy chair, brought an ache right to the core of my chest. He was the one person that I was truly going to miss. I would miss him with every fiber of my being.

I walked over and lounged back on the arm of his chair.

"How was dinner?" he asked, smiling like he already knew the answer.

I made a face at him, and he chuckled. I was going to miss that sound too. I sat there with my dad, thinking of all the things that he was going to miss. One day I really would get married, and he wouldn't be there to walk me down the aisle. One day I would have kids, and they wouldn't get to know their grandpa. They couldn't. Once I left here, I'd have to cover my tracks. I'd be gone for good. I'd forever be an outsider, and the thought of never seeing Dad again was heart-wrenching.

I leaned over and gave him a big hug.

"What was that for?" he asked.

I got up and stood next to his chair. "I love you, Dad."

He smiled. "I love you too, baby girl. Go get some sleep."

*****

The next day, when my parents were out shopping, I began to pack. I pulled out an old duffle bag and started filling it with necessities. Once it was full, I carried it downstairs and placed it in the trunk of my car. On the way back to my room, I grabbed a couple of sheets of paper and a pen from my dad's office. I wasn't going to be able to tell anyone why I was leaving or where I was going, but the least I could do was give them as much of an explanation as I could.

After packing another tote full of my things, I sat down to write my letters.

I wrote the first to Marcus. I simply told him that I could not marry him because I didn't love him, and because my heart belonged to another. I ended the short scrawl with, *I wish you and Noel all the best. If you love her, marry her and never look back. Do something for yourself for once and find the happiness that you deserve.* I actually meant it.

The second letter was more difficult to write:

Dear Mom & Dad,
I'm sorry to leave this way, but you gave me no choice. I will not marry a man I don't love. Don't worry about Marcus, he will be fine with Noel. He has been for a while now. I met a wonderful man who loves me and accepts me for who I am. All of me. He is brilliant and talented, and I'm sure if the situation were different you would both love him. I do. I love him more than I can say, and he loves me just as much. And I deserve to be loved. Please understand that I'm not running away to be with him. I'm leaving because, after loving

him, I could never be the daughter you expect. I'm doing this for me. Please don't try to find me. I will contact you when the time is right. For now, I need you to let me go. You will always be in my thoughts. May the pack flourish and be safe without me.

All my love,
Lily

I couldn't face my parents, so I spent the remainder of the evening in my room. After sitting in my chair, staring at the clock while my legs shook with anticipation and nerves, it was finally time. I picked up my tote bag and the two letters and quietly walked downstairs. I placed the letters on the table by the front door and picked up my purse and my keys. With my hand on the doorknob, I took a moment to look around at the only home I had ever lived in. Then I left.

I drove quickly to the main road, but every few seconds I glanced into the rearview mirror to make sure I wasn't being followed. It wasn't until I'd crossed the estate's property line that I could actually breathe again. I'd made it out and no one was after me.

When I saw Paul's Camaro parked a little way down the road, I let out a sigh of relief and smiled. I pulled my car over onto the side of the road where my parents would be able to find it easily and grabbed my bags from the trunk.

Paul saw me running toward him with my bags slung hastily over my shoulders, and he hurried to meet me. I could feel my face flush as he lifted me off the ground and swung me around, bags and all.

"Paul, we have to hurry," I said, worried that someone would see us.

"I don't care. I want to see your face. This is the beginning of our lives together. I want to remember exactly what you looked like right now, in this moment," he said.

I couldn't help myself; I dropped my bags and threw my arms around him. As our lips met, I knew without a shadow of a doubt that this man would be forever mine.

Two minutes later, the estate and my life there was just a speck in the rearview mirror.

Chapter 17

I rolled out of bed extra early and dragged myself into the little restroom of our tiny, 490 square-foot apartment. It was kind of like living in an air-conditioned, two-car garage with a bathroom attached, but I couldn't care less about the size. Yes, it was small, but I liked to think of it as cozy, and it was what we could afford. I absolutely loved it. It was perfect. It felt like home, a place that I could just be me.

In hindsight, maybe the real reason I clung so desperately to my relationship with Marcus for as long as I did, why I'd tried so hard to be the perfect daughter of the enforcer, was because I'd never felt like I was really the person everyone expected me to be. I'd always felt so out of place, like I was never truly part of the pack. Now I knew what it meant to truly be me, how it felt to have someone truly love me. All of me. I'd never been happier.

In only three short weeks, Paul and I had started a new life here in Austin, Texas. In addition to his gig that would start soon, he landed a job at a local record store called Tracks, and within a few days of arriving I found a job at a cute little indie bookstore. On my next day off I planned on heading over to Austin Community College to get some information on registration and school loans, but before I could do that I needed to make sure it was safe to use my real name.

I had to wait for the right moment. There was only one person I'd ever really trusted in our pack. He'd always said that he wanted the best for me, and all I could do was hope he truly meant it.

When I knew that Dad would be the only one home, I made the call from a payphone down the street.

"Hello," he answered, and I froze. Unexpected tears sprang into my eyes the moment I heard his familiar, deep voice. "Hello? Who is this?" he demanded.

I tried to speak, but the words just wouldn't come.

"Lily, baby? Is that you?" His voice automatically shifted from that of our pack enforcer to that of the loving father I'd grown up adoring.

"Hi, Dad," I answered, my words strained and barely audible.

"Oh, baby, thank God! I'm so glad you called."

I had to pull it together. I needed to know if I was safe or if I'd just made my biggest mistake yet by calling. I took a deep breath and asked, "Dad, listen, I'm sorry and I miss you so much. But I'm really happy here, and I'm not coming home. I just need to make sure that we are safe, that Marcus isn't looking for us."

The silence stretched on.

"Dad?"

"Lily, listen to me. Please know it kills me to say this, because I miss you more than you'll ever know. But if you are happy, truly happy, then do not come back. You can't ever come back. I will make sure no one ever comes looking for you," he said.

"You will?"

"Of course I will. You are my baby, and all I've ever wanted is for you to be happy. I'm sorry I was so blind. I just wanted to believe so badly that your mother and I were doing the right thing. I'd never say it to another living soul, but honey, I'm so proud of you. Go live the life you deserve, just please be careful. I love you. Always remember that wherever you are. Remember that I love you."

"I love you too, Dad," I started, and I wanted to say so much more, but the phone clicked and the line went dead. My father was gone, and the realization of that brought me to my knees.

I dropped the phone, and it dangled from the cord as I sank to ground and sobbed. I was incredibly sad, but I also couldn't believe it. Paul and I were going to make it. My dad was going to keep us safe. And he was proud of me for being who I am.

Everything looked safe and clear for the rest of our life together.

＊＊＊＊＊

After a late night, the last thing I wanted to do was haul my dog-tired butt out of bed, but I needed to take my first official trip to the grocery store alone. Paul had car-pooled to Tracks this morning so I could pick up a few things before I had to go to work.

The clock was ticking, so I hurried to get dressed and high-tailed it to the local Foodtown. My first stop was the produce aisle, and this might sound totally lame, but I felt so grown up, which was sort of odd, being that a few weeks ago I was planning a wedding and had a house with a fully decorated nursery awaiting me yet it wasn't until this moment that I actually felt like an adult. There was just something about picking out fresh veggies that screamed, *Hey, look at me. I'm living on my own and I plan on cooking real food in my very own kitchen.*

Yes, I was being silly, but I couldn't help it. I was happy. Paul loved me, and there wasn't a single part of me that regretted my decision. My life was working out just like it was supposed to. With each day that passed, our worries lessened that the pack might show up out of the blue and try to force me to go back. After I'd talked to my dad, I started to believe they really were going to let me go. Either that, or they had no idea where I went. Just to be safe, I used cash only and didn't plan on opening my own bank account for a while.

I followed my grocery list to a T, and by the time I crossed off the last item on the page my basket was full. Just before I headed to the checkout area, however, I remembered that I was almost out of face wash, so I took a quick detour to the toiletries section.

Looking up at the signs overhead, I searched for the one that listed soap…then did a double-take when two words in particular caught my eye. *Holy Mother of God! Feminine hygiene!* I stood there frozen in the middle of the main aisle. Staring at the sign hanging from the ceiling, I tried to think back. How long had it been since I'd had my last period?

There was only one answer. Too damn long.

Suddenly I needed to sit down, and I did. I sank to the ground next to my basket, hung my head in my hands, and tried desperately not to have a panic attack on the dingy floor of Foodtown.

Wait. How could this be? I'd been careful. Each and every time I'd made sure we were careful. Maybe I wasn't pregnant. Maybe it was just the stress of everything that had transpired over the last month or so. Surely that could be it. But one way or the other I needed to be sure.

I dragged my shaking body up off the floor and wiped away the tears I hadn't even realized had fallen, and I reminded myself to breathe in and out as I wobbled over to the shelf containing the pregnancy tests. With a spinning head, I couldn't read the tiny print on the back of the boxes, so I picked out three different brands and tossed them in the basket.

Somehow I must have checked out, loaded the car, and driven home. I wasn't sure how I even got back to the apartment. Everything was one big blur. As I unpacked and put away the groceries, I placed the tests on the counter.

After everything was in its proper place, I stood in the kitchen and stared at the three little boxes. They might very well change my life forever. I glanced at the clock on the wall. I had to be at work in an hour. I also had to know.

Completely numb, I grabbed all three boxes and a plastic cup and stumbled to the bathroom. I almost laughed when I thought that this kind of felt like doing a science experiment, which just went to show my mental state because there was not one single amusing thing about an eighteen-year-old runaway taking a pregnancy test.

My eyes shifted back and forth between the second hand on my watch and the result screens on the tests. It was the longest three minutes in the history of man, but finally the results appeared, and I grabbed the directions, read and re-read the tiny print, and then sank to the floor once again. Tears poured from my eyes as I sobbed uncontrollably.

How can this be? How am I going to tell Paul? Paul! Shit-shit-shit!

I rose up from the floor, dashed into the kitchen, and flung open the door to the pantry. Inside hung a calendar with both of our work schedules penciled in. I pulled it off the tack that held it in place and flipped it back to May. I counted the weeks, recounted the days, and then found a pen to do the math on paper. The numbers didn't add up. There was absolutely no way that the baby inside me was Paul's, which could only mean one thing.

I was carrying Marcus Walker's baby.

Chapter 18

My head pounded as I sat on the couch in our apartment waiting for Paul to get home. From the second I saw the hot pink line appear in the positive window of the first test, I'd been in a constant state of shock. I didn't freak out. I didn't cry anymore. I'd just methodically packed a bag knowing that once I told Paul he would want me to leave.

I called in sick to work and then called the bus station. There was a bus leaving tonight at 9:15 that made a stop in Santa Fe. From there I could call Marcus. No one on the estate would be thrilled to accept me back into the pack, but once they found out that I was carrying their alpha's baby, they would do it. They'd have to. And Marcus, even though he hated me, would marry me.

I had been sitting in the same spot for more than four hours by the time I heard Paul walking up the stairs to our apartment. I held my breath as I listened to him slip his key into the lock, and my heart nearly stopped as the knob turned and the door opened. Seeing his face, knowing that I would never be able to hold him again after today, sent me falling headfirst into reality, and the built-up tears flooded my eyes.

Paul dropped his keys and ran over. He knelt down before me and took both my hands in his. "Lillian, what is it? What's wrong?"

When I didn't answer, he began to search the room with his eyes. I knew the exact moment when he saw my packed bag. "Damn it, Lillian, tell me what happened!"

"Sit down, Paul," I said, managing to pull myself together a bit.

"Not until you tell me why you have a bag packed. Are you leaving me, Lillian?"

I reached for his hand, and he let me take it. I could tell that he didn't want to give in, but he sat anyway.

"I have to go back to the estate," I told him.

"Why? Did someone find us? Did they threaten you?" Paul asked in a panic.

"It's not like that. No one has found us."

"I don't understand, Lillian. Why would you want to go back there?" Tears darkened his beautiful blue eyes.

"Because I'm pregnant," I whispered.

"You're what?"

I took a shaky, deep breath and repeated, "I'm pregnant."

Paul's initial reaction shattered my heart into a million pieces. His smile was real, raw emotion; he was ecstatic. Then, it was like I could see him doing the same math in his head that I had done earlier, and his gorgeous smile started to fade. He stood up and began to walk out of the room. He was about to disappear into the kitchen when he turned to me and said, "I need a minute. Do *not* leave, okay?"

I nodded. What else could I do? I had just ruined his life. I bet he wished he could go back in time to that music festival and do things differently. If I left now, he would recover. He may be sad and hurt, but he would move on. He would find someone else, and one day he would have his own family. He would have everything he deserved.

All at once my stomach clenched, and I ran into our tiny bathroom. I wasn't sure if my first case of morning sickness had struck or if it was purely from stress, but I was vomiting in the middle of the most important conversation of my life. Whatever it was, it was definitely karma.

After I brushed my teeth and washed my face, I stood in front of the mirror staring at a girl I hardly recognized anymore. I wasn't sure what to say to her.

I walked back into the living room, and Paul was leaning against the wall near the kitchen. He had a beer in one hand and a glass of water in the other. We both walked toward the couch, and he handed me the water.

I thanked him without meeting his eyes. I thought he was going to sit beside me, but he didn't. Instead, he picked up my bag and carried it into the bedroom. I sat there confused.

Paul came back in and knelt in front of me. "Do you really love me, Lillian?" he asked.

"You know I do, but—"

"No buts. Just answer my question. Do you love me?"

"Yes."

"Are you happy here?"

"Of course."

"Then stay," he said.

"But what about Marcus? The baby?" I asked.

"Call him. Tell him that you're pregnant. After the baby's born, you can work out some kind of custody agreement. People do that all the time," he said rationally.

That solution might have been perfectly rational for a human, but not for a werewolf. I tried to explain to Paul that things in a pack worked differently.

"If I call and tell Marcus that I'm pregnant with his child, he would be here tonight. He would force me back on the estate," I explained.

Paul furrowed his brow. With conviction in his voice he responded, "He can't do that. I wouldn't let him."

I so loved this man, but he didn't understand. I was carrying Marcus's heir. There would be no way in hell he would share custody, much less allow another man, a human, to raise that child. If Marcus—or any pack member for that matter—knew this baby was his, I would be married to Marcus and living in that house on the estate in the blink of an eye.

"I don't think I have many options, Paul. And I'm not being dramatic when I say that Marcus would have you killed and drag me back if he found out. There will be no 'talking it out,'" I said.

Paul moved to sit next to me on the couch. "I don't want you to leave," he said, staring at the wall in front of him. "Ever."

"I don't want to leave," I admitted.

"I'm in love with you, Lillian."

"I've never doubted that. And I love you more than I thought was even possible," I said.

"You have to do what you think is right, but if you stay, I will love you and your child for the rest of my life," he said as he turned to look at me.

"You would do that? You would love this baby?" I asked, overcome.

"As my own," he swore.

As soon as the words left his lips, I crawled onto his lap and showered kisses all over his face.

"Does this mean you're going to stay?" he asked.

"Forever," I whispered, loving his smile. And I knew that I would. I would be with him forever, and there was no place I'd rather be.

"Lillian," Paul said between those passionate kisses that I loved so much. "Marry me."

Chapter 19

The next few months went by so quickly that sometimes it felt as though I was barely keeping my head above water. The same day I told Paul I was pregnant I also told him that I wouldn't marry him. But the truth was that I did *want* to marry him. I just didn't want to feel as though we were getting married just because I was expecting. After my time with Marcus, I couldn't agree to any marriage of obligation. I told Paul that if he still wanted to marry me after all the sleepless nights and dirty diapers to ask me again. He seemed satisfied with that, and since then our love for each other grew right along with my belly.

Paul's career really took off. He'd sold his first song back in October and a few more since. With the extra money we moved from our tiny one-bedroom to a tiny two-bedroom, and it probably wouldn't be long before Paul could quit his job at the record store and write full-time.

He brought home a giant box one day and spent three hours in the baby's room. He wouldn't let me in, not even once. Finally, he came out looking very proud of himself, and when I saw what he did I burst into tears. Paul was used to all my crying by then, so he knew they were happy tears. And the crib was absolutely perfect!

My first semester as a college student at ACC was incredible. I absolutely loved my classes and decided to major in computer science. I couldn't believe that I'd ever considered not going to college, and I refused to let my pregnancy stop me. I was really good at school, too: straight A's. Whenever I thought back to my life on the estate, and to the future I would have had there, I was doubly grateful for my one moment of bravery—and to Tiffany for ditching me for that hottie. I often found myself wondering if she ever made it out of Red Ridge like she planned. For her sake I hoped she had, and that maybe we would find each other again someday.

Paul was playing his usual Thursday-night gig when the contractions started. I tried to call the bar, but no one was answering the phone. I was just about to bang on our neighbor's door to beg for help when I heard Paul's key slip into the front lock. It was 3:00 a.m. and the contractions were only four minutes apart. I was flooded with relief, but poor Paul freaked out!

It probably didn't help matters that I was lying in the middle of the living room floor with a bed sheet and a sheet of plastic underneath me. We were having this baby at home since there was no way I could have a nonhuman baby in a regular hospital; there was just no way to hide the fact that I wasn't human. They'd know something was off the second they took my temperature, and the complications that could come with having a baby at home without a doctor were nothing compared to what could happen if someone found out about werewolves. Plus, I was healthy, so there was really no reason to think that everything wouldn't go as planned.

At least that was what I kept telling myself.

As soon as Paul saw me, he slammed the door and slid to his knees in front of me. "Holy shit, Lillian. Maybe this isn't such a good idea. There's still time to get to a hospital."

"Paul, you know we can't. Look, we've planned for this. You've researched it for months. You know what you're doing. You can do this! But you have to calm down." He looked like he was the one in labor. Sweat dripped down the sides of his face, and he was breathing erratically as he hurried to the kitchen to wash his hands and get everything ready.

By the time my body was telling me it was time to push, Paul was handling the pressure like a champ, and it was me doing the freaking out. I screamed so loud that I was sure the police would be banging on our door any minute, but thankfully the neighbors didn't seem to notice. Paul assured me over and over that I was doing fine and that everything would be okay, and it all passed by in a blurry haze of excruciating pain, creative cussing, and a sudden rush of relief when we finally became the proud parents of a healthy baby boy.

He was beautiful. He was perfect.

With tears in my eyes I begged, "We can never tell him the truth. Promise me that he'll never know. He can never know that I was only eighteen when he was born. That I ran away from home. He can never know that you're not his biological father. Promise me."

Paul leaned in and kissed me tenderly, careful not to disturb the precious new life in my arms. "I'm his father. I always will be. That I can promise. And don't worry. Everything will work out. From this moment on, you are twenty-one. A twenty-one-year-old woman who decided to leave home of her own free will. Don't worry, baby. It will be our secret."

A few hours later I woke up from a small nap and saw the most beautiful sight I had ever seen. Paul was sitting in the recliner rocking Aiden.

Aiden Wright. Our son.

*****

Six months later we were standing in the doorway of Aiden's bedroom watching our little man sleep, and out of nowhere Paul dragged me into the room. He said he wanted our son to be there for this in his "own little way."

There, right there in the middle of the nursery, Paul asked me to marry him again. With overwhelming love in his eyes he pledged, "All the sleepless nights and dirty diapers in the world couldn't keep me from asking you this a million times over. Marry me, Lillian Michaels. You are the strongest, most beautiful woman I've ever known, and nothing would make me happier than to call you my wife."

He took my hands, sank down to his knee, and he held out a beautiful ring.

This time I said yes.

Epilogue

Christmas morning, 2012

Blinking back tears, I turn away from the window and from the memories of the past. I knew coming back here would be hard, but I never dreamed that it would take this much out of me. I know I did the right thing, though. Leaving this place all those years ago was the bravest decision I ever made. Coming back was the hardest. It was still right.

I wipe my eyes and follow the smell of bacon, pancakes, and fresh coffee downstairs. When I reach the bottom step, I can see everyone gathered around the island in the kitchen. Paul is standing over the stove, trying to keep the bacon grease from spattering his arms. Those arms. Those beautifully tattooed arms that really once saved my life.

Aiden is pouring a glass of orange juice for his mate, Teagan. She's a sweet girl who will make my baby very happy. He loves her. That makes me happy. Regardless of whether or not he becomes the alpha here, he will never have to choose between loyalty and love. He will get to have both.

Paul and our daughter Alli laugh as he tries to a stick a piece of burnt bacon into her mouth. As he wrestles her into a headlock, he sees me. My knees still go all wobbly when he smiles at me that way. That rock-star smile lights up his face and reaches all the way up into those swimming-pool-blue eyes of his.

"Help me, Mom," Alli screeches as she tries to wrestle away, which she could easily do if she really wanted, what with her werewolf strength and all.

Seeing them together and knowing that our children grew up loved and cherished made all the suffering and heartbreak of my past worth it. I gave up my life here nineteen years ago for a new one full of happiness and unconditional love with Paul, and I have never, ever regretted it. Whatever comes next with the boys and Marcus, no matter what our future holds, I never will.

AUTHORS' NOTE

1994 was undoubtedly an epic year for Lillian and the Red Ridge Pack, but it was pretty big for the rest of us, too. Bill Clinton was in his second year as president. Millions were glued to their television sets watching as O.J. Simpson took the L.A. police on one wild ride. We all said hello to a couple of new television shows that would become forever iconic, *Friends* and *ER*. And some of the biggest movies ever, *Pulp Fiction* and *Forrest Gump*, hit the silver screen. We also had to say goodbye to a young, brilliant musician who changed music forever, Nirvana's Kurt Cobain.

1994 was NOT a good year for fashion, but the music was HOT! Here are some of the year's best!

- "Whatta Man" – Salt-N-Pepa

- "Hero" – Mariah Carey

- "Regulate" – Warren G and Nate Dogg

- "Here Comes the Hotstepper" – Ini Kamoze

- "Keep Ya Head Up" – 2Pac

- "Crazy" – Aerosmith

- "Linger" – Cranberries

- "I Swear" – All-4-One

- "Fantastic Voyage" – Coolio

- "Whoop!" – Tag Team

- "Found Out About You" – Gin Blossoms

- "Tootsee Roll" – 69 Boyz

- "Mr. Jones" – Counting Crows

- "Loser" – Beck

- "Gin & Juice" – Snoop Dogg

You're welcome!
—Staci Weber, St. Agnes Academy, *Class of 1994!* Go Tigers!
—Sara Dailey, Sam Rayburn High School, *Class of 1998!* Go Texans!

ABOUT THE AUTHORS

Sara Dailey and Staci Weber have been friends and co-workers for nearly ten years. They both have a wild thing for romance novels, sweet white wine, and men with tattoos. They both live in League City, TX, with their husbands and kids. *Born of Lies* is their fourth novel together.

www.ingramcontent.com/pod-product-compliance
Lightning Source LLC
Chambersburg PA
CBHW071414170626
46811CB00003B/1398

* 9 7 8 1 9 4 1 2 6 0 5 2 4 *